The Place Where Someone Ate a Flower

The Place Where Someone Ate a Flower

Sexuality of the novel, or, in other words, an obsessive study of the phenomenon of sexuality and the nature of its freedom within a single family over two generations

SEAD MAHMUTEFENDIC

Library of Congress Control Number: 2020908124

ISBN:	Hardcover	978-1-9845-9488-4
	Softcover	978-1-9845-9487-7
	eBook	978-1-9845-9486-0

Print information available on the last page.

Rev. date: 05/11/2020

To order additional copies of this book, contact:
Xlibris
800-056-3182
www.Xlibrispublishing.co.uk
Orders@Xlibrispublishing.co.uk
813419

CONTENTS

I record a few notes about an event that, no doubt, speaks of the secrets of our loneliness.

Indeed, as I write this, not without a hint of some success, I try to delicately go into details, mimicking the tiny blurs as the most ravenous enemy I have discovered in them.

How in fact this is the way that things like this appear before my very eyes.

To hark back, madam Aman Fanny said that she would buy flowers by herself, even though she had too much on her plate at home.

This book is dedicated to the women in my life, without whose support and love this book would not have been possible.

This book is dedicated to my mother, my best friend, who was endowed with intense loyalty and perseverance, a heart as big as her words and a wicked sense of humor. She possessed profundity, intelligence and strength beyond her years.

And lastly, it is dedicated to Valentina, Marija and Kasima, my three wives with lion hearts and ancient, baby souls.

Every mistake a man can make is driven by sex.
From the American movie "The Human Stain"

BELIEVE IT OR not, some people are just not made to be faithful! It sounds like a good excuse for anyone who likes to 'two-time', but scientists have found a **gene** that raises the odds of cheating on a partner.

They claim that when a woman or man with this particular gene has an affair, they get the same chemical rush as a gambler whose luck has changed or an alcoholic savoring a drink.

Researchers quizzed 180 young women and men about their attitude towards relationships and tested them for a **gene**called DRD4, which affectsdopamine levels in the brain.

One quarter of those with the gene in question are more than twice as likely to be unfaithful, and when they cheated, they cheated with more than one person.

A researcher at the University of New York said that these results suggest it is possible for a person with the **gene** in question to feel committed to a partner, but still feel the need to cheat on them.

> We found that individuals with a certain variant of the DRD4 gene are more likely to cheat and have uncommitted sex – said the researcher.

Scientific discovery: the DRD4 gene is responsible for cheating and adultery

CHAPTER ONE

Halted at the Top of the Bounce

PREFACE

TODAY, DESPITE A developed system of communications, there are "cultural biases", which are often adopted from the West, without sufficient scrutiny.

The Bosniak fantasy in particular, since it has not been the subject of contestation, has not evolved in the segment of anti-rationalist and anti-clerical character (dark and spooky).

Unlike in the West, where through fantasy one immersed oneself in the forbidden zone(once again the motif of anxiety, in anticipation of punishment), in the Bosniak literature such "zones" are rare, and mystery, with the aura of ambiguity that it entails, does not have so much a role to scare as to discover another "face" of the world, as "real" as the one we perceive. It is more about discovering a higher order of things, a universal secret that encompasses both tangible and intangible existence. It is not aimed at effect or shock but is aimed at spreading the *weltanschauung* or worldview. It is fantasy with no signal, no intimation. It is, so to speak, of the "epiphanic" nature, in which the epiphany or the revelation of experience is an instrument of understanding and cognition of the world.

Unlike the Western conception, where the notion of a mirror is often present, as well as entering the mirror as into the "other-worldly", into another plane, not only one plane or a plane the edges of which are so precisely defined exists here, it would rather be more appropriate to talk about the relationship between the micro-and macrocosm similar to the relationship that exists between the acorn and the entire oak forest contained in it.

The relationship between the "other-worldly" and "this-worldly" can be heightened by comparing two symbolic characters: Prometheus and Orpheus. Specifically, they represent two (opposite) possibilities in resolving this relationship. While Prometheus is a solar, active personality who, from matter, from the physical world, struggles with transcendence (which is opposed to him), Orpheus succeeds with his songs to penetrate both "that" and "this" world without any struggle. He communicates with both the tangible and the intangible world. Are those vibrations the “word” that was in the beginning? As the daughter of myth, literature has certainly preserved that possibility of traversing and penetrating through various layers and planes of existence. In the *Thousand and One Nights* stories, for instance, storytelling is believed to be able to change the cruelest intentions of a ruler. In these stories of mine the same idea is present, as well as music and narrative within everyday life.

What is the idea I want to intimate with this Preface? More important is the attempt *to understand* than*to know,* and the most important is the attempt of the reader to transpose himself or herself *into* the described world.

Can closely connected people live together on the basis of absolute honesty? The more they seek to reveal their inner selves to each other, the opaqueer, unknowable they become to one another. Two psychological components work together: the obsessive urge for sincerity, bordering on exhibitionism, and the knowledgefor the insurmountable loneliness of every soul that borders on despair.

Who knows, perhaps in this book there is a sign which will move you to the depths of your soul, to the world where reality is being formed the way you want it, to the space illuminated by some magnificent blueness as long as you firmly close your eyes and immerse your dream into darkness. The only thing death can do to the soul is to have it forget that it has already lived.

INTRODUCTION

THE WHITE CEILING was ominously dropping towards me. The spider was sitting on a cup of coffee before deciding to go down and suck on the dregs after me. I was looking at it sideways. My muscles hurt from the oblique angle. I was thinking: if I reach out, I have to be quick to cover the top of the cup with my palm to close the passage so it doesn't take off. I have always hated any of my efforts gooing down the drain. Then I would probably feel its tentacles touching me to ask or warn me to remove my palm and let it come out of the cup.

At that moment, someone knocked on the door. I was still keeping my palm on the top of the cup. The knocking repeated.

Who's at the door?

What does the one standing in front of it have to tell me? What news do they bring me? I'm afraid that if I open it, I will see a gun pointed at my head. So, I resolutely rumbled: "I'm not here!"

Instead of the shot, through the closed door I could hear restless pacing. I was trying to look at myself through the eyes of the bitch on the other side of the door.

- Maks! –indeed, some bitch called me by name.

I thought this could be some kind of a trap. Carefully, very carefully, I searched for a knife under the rug. While I was still cursing God for fumbling for the lock so much, the door in front of me stretched wide open. And at the door I saw a broad with a revolver in her hand. She put it in her tracksuit pocket, looking at me wickedly, like: "I came to kill you too, son of a bitch!"

I quickly looked away. I pretended I was looking at a bunch of flowers and not a real gun. The most important thing was to remain cool.

You answered the door without even blinking or raising your eyebrows. You have so many eyebrows; if only a part of them you raised at me, but you didn't, her gaze was telling me.

This is quite OK. It's time for me to die. I somehow felt like I had just completely broken off with my life. Calmly, bathed and toothbrushedbefore bedtime.

Like a fairy-tale ghost, my whippersnapper-beauty from the bus blew into the flat. She didn't have a broom, but she brought with her those two devilish eyes like two ripe blackberries. Two-thirds of her body were her legs, and one third consisted of her head, torso and arms, not counting her panties, if she had them at all. If she did not have them, then it was only one quarter.

She slipped her slender body and her doe's gaitinto the room.

- What do you want? –Icouldn't think of a better question, and yet her tongue was already jumping and darting within her open mouth.

- I want you to love me!

- Squirrel, stop hanging onto my neck, you will suffocate me! It's Wednesday evening, and it's a day for rumination.

- The two of us are a terrific team, huh, Maks, old chap? You have always been full of shit, which made half-witted me stick to you like glue, may I be damned for having set my eyes on you!

My brain was confidentially urging me to fly out of here. The poor guy took great pains so that she wouldn't hear it. The poor brain seemed to have had enough for today. The poor guy didn't feel like sleeping, just like lying awake.

He was lying on the bare white sheet as dark as an ant. He thought about how he would undress her slowly, how he would feel every pore of his body igniting, how millions of miniscule craters of his complexion would begin secreting sweat, and she would be white, naked, serious, elegant, motionless, gently taking the stockings off while kneeling at his feet. He would watch her hands descending, descending along those legs so white. And she was already in bed and she would see that, all white and perfect, she was lying behind the tulle curtains, and she would hear him say, take it off. She would take it off, and he would say quickly, quickly, and he would see how, so tall, she contorts to remove her blouse and moves her feet fast, fast, and the shoes would silently fall on the carpet. A bulky tanned body would get on the sheets in silence. His body would be a torch. They would then embrace, smell each other, sweat and the two of them would turn into knots. White arms, four arms, two fuzzy and two bare, plump and thin lips, taut rough nipples, small, crystal, pellucid and soft, suntanned thighs and the limpid ones with blue veins, deep black, straight hairs, and those golden, curly ones.

She came quite close to him, looked at him with beautiful eyes that resembled two ripe blackberries, and wordlessly wrapped her braids, which she plaited her hair into, around his neck. She then tied them at his nape and tightened them into a knot until their lips met. Then she pushed him onto bed, straddled the bed and him in bed. He thought: it will be incomprehensible, but wonderful. It will be snowing outside as if the sky were showering the earth with silent white words, and everything will happen as if she were falling alongside the snow from endless heights and in a single direction, without pulling back even for a moment, just as the snow cannot go back to the skies, to purity.

You do realize what people need if they could come to an agreement –shetold him with a voice that sounded like pearls being scattered. – Love!And man is unhappy just because he is stupid and does not know about it.

He watched her from below: "My dearest, you have quite a shallow smile, so whenever you smile, I must end up stranded on your nose, and your cheeks are the waves. I will never allow that smile of yours to heal, like the wound in the water, neither quickly nor ever.

- Will our child have already been born when we see each other again? –she asked him.

These were words like the recent scattered pearls, but they were now completely still.

- If you plan on us having a baby, watch what I eat. Always eat the opposite. Those who want to make a baby must not eat the same food – he replied. - You will count my teeth with your tongue, you will have your upper lip salty with fear, and the lower one a tad bitter, and the heart that beats as if stolen. I will then feel your eyelashes scratching my cheeks and your hip against my belly. I will be full of your saliva and, with the member that you will erect, I will impregnate you with such vehemence so we will never be quite clear about which one of us our son belongs to.

All complications in life arise from the collision of feeling and passions. Feelings and passions are the requisites of happiness and cannot be separated, for passion without feeling is a vice, and feeling without passion is an illness.

Snapshot of a landscape of the onegetting up and going to the corner

I WANT TO emphasize that I do not perform any ritual either before myself or before others by this writing, and that in moments of honest confession I place my open palm over my heart. Obviously, I do not see any signs of loneliness that the finger of fate would have destined for me, but – I think that it is so – on the contrary, to seek out a connection with what could explain the invisible chain between our face, which everyone remembers well and, supposedly, know us therefore, and our personal outlines, by which they form an idea of us but most often do not understand us. Should I later call this a correspondence in which there is always something colorless and weak, or a practical virtue, which in a sense is inherent to loyalty and confidentiality?

In the introduction to this story, I dare instruct you how to approach it, its chapters, and how and where to read it. Approach each chapter as one weaker reflective poem with a strong lyric structure. And if you have the opportunity to do so, read it in moments of loneliness; somewhere in the mighty and serene solitudes, or perhaps in a crowd, in cheerful company in need of something completely, completely something safe. You have the power to overcome the impossible evil forces of nature that are stronger than human beings who do not love you.

And one more thing: in this story, my name will be Maks, or shorter - J.M.

There is something I would not even try to explain at this point and what I would have to spare you from. I purposely say: would have to, and not: would need to, because some things, under needfulness, put off the comprehensibility of their apocalyptic essence, of course, if doubting it would constitute a burden judging from the life we led until that moment. Consequently, a created disposition is required for a mutual understanding of that mutual distinction, that is, between must and needfulness, to which then no reasonable person ever denies them their possibilities.

Whenever he would return home, J.M. would be slightly smiling, but he did it so discreetly that, if in his presence, one might rather think of it as being a sign of melancholy, to which he was extremely inclined. But his enigmatic smile was far from uniting the shallowness and gloom of the fervidness, which, in all likelihood, was behind it all. More than usual, he liked having someone close to him whom he would gently grasp by the hand, by the shoulder, just enough to feel the closeness of a living thing that would arouse the joy in him which, nevertheless, would not be completely devoid of fear.

Snapshot of a landscape of the grigri against everything

WHILE IN THE anteroom, still excited by today's laborious day, he truly wanted to satisfy his curiosity, while at the same time restraining himself and giving this personal and intimate matter a dignified form. What had happened today interfered with his solitary job. He was afraid he would explode. Is he going to be able to keep his emotions to himself only? He was unable to reason, which meant that he had no foothold against the immense joy after they, having informed him that he had been admitted to the Academy of Sciences and Arts as its youngest member, elated him so much so that he could hardly restrain himself from presumptuously holding his head high.

True, he had often thought about this moment before, since he did not even know how he would behave if the proposal to admit him were rejected. Terrified that this might happen to him, he prepared himself to be ready, as a loser, to rise above it somehowand not be kept on a leash by failure and ridicule, and not to go to extremes to such extent so as to endanger his dignity of a citizen and scholar. Due to all of this, he shifted his shoulders in his own way under his coat, making a grimace at the corner of his lips, twitching it down. In doing so, he expressed a doubt that he was still bored by these light-minded things.

The anteroom was quiet.

It was a call for an earthquake

J.M'S HEART WAS now swollen with deep emotion, so he had no reason to be ashamed, the proof of which was his yellow and dry complexion, which replaced his natural dark complexion day after day. Even though he was trying to think academically, and not personally, he noticed that there was so much such naivety and such responsibility in his attitude, making his inner relation towards that notion more theoretical than practical, because he was deeply aware how much his mood was conditioned, but that did not stop him from behaving nicely. Even his inner lamentations ceased, which made him excited and angry. Was that why his eyes were slightly more bulging and his cheeks sunken? Anyway, he wasn't quite convinced, so he shook a bit angrily and mumbled to himself: “Well then, we look as if we’re getting a bit faintfrom having too much to drink!”

And then, all of a sudden, he burst into tears, let them stream down his cheeks, and moved towards the interior of the anteroom, but he immediately found an excuse before himself that this clear liquid flowed so abundantly and bitterly everywhere in the world at each and every moment, so that this earthly valley got its poetic name. Hence this mucus and protein led him toa nerve convulsion, to penetrating pain – physical and mental pain. His aching lips began crying, his mouth sagging and sadly agape, but at the same moment, that suffering expression would flash with lustfulness, the inclination of his head would turn into naughtiness, and his lips, still open, would smirk lecherously.

Snapshot of a landscape on a given death

SO FAR, I have destroyed one hundred lives and yet have not been able to escape from myself. I would try it even now if I could, but certain frailty does not allow me. I simply don't want to harm anyone; perhaps only myself, but that vortex usually painfully engulfs the one who is with me, myself included.

The futility with which Aman Fanny was changing the thickness of the glass

AS HE WAS watching Aman Fanny, J.M's heart sank even more for some dark reasons. It seemed, no doubt, to be the case. The girl kept looking at him, by turns shooting glances at him, at Anđela, at the sight of what Aman Fanny was looking at on the outer side of the stranger's thigh.

J.M. saw that blond hair jutting out from beneath the scarf that wrapped her head. He wanted to hug her, but he couldn't because it seemed out of place to him now. He wanted to leave there, take a walk, get some air, but to come back again and to listen to that horrific story until the end.

On the other hand, similar to all family dreams, J.M. was not quite sure that he had touched upon another question, which could trigger a confession that not only could not ennoble and exalt him but might excite him so much so as to make him angry.

At whom? At himself? At Aman Fanny?

God knows to whose address he could direct his anger, which was surging at such a speed as if something like a spring of a broken clock had been taken out of the brain of a hashish-entranced creature.

Will he have the patience to express his fears before these unfamiliar people and the patience of not having to express his feelings in words in his disconnected manner, in which he really succeeded completely thanks to the general impression of his personality. He placed both hands with palms down on the table surface, raising his pointy forefinger as if wanting to tell them that what he heard was very important and to express his tense expectation that it should not be communicated or interpreted publicly. With concealed anxiety that made him feel his pulse pounding in his jugular vein, he made a great deal of effort to keep it unnoticeable; with rat-like dilated pupils, black as charcoal, and the success of camouflaging it served him shamelessly. These shocks were in each of the present beings, for they were not confined solely to the one who was creating them with his story and with his cold wariness. J.M. was simply competing, unable to fully overcome his excitement. Still, not only did their cheeks glow and their eyes widen and shine with the tension caused by Aman Fanny's story, but a state was created that could be called a tension, by their excitement that would not allow them to take a breather, by their almost painful focus on this horrific story.

Yet what ensued, a moment or two later, no one could have guessed; Mr. J.M. got sick and almost fell unconscious.

Snapshot of love at the drowning man's straw

THEY WERE SILENT for a while, but J.M. did that just because he felt comfortable this way, because it seemed to him that any word uttered now would put him in spiritual and emotional danger if he were not only to utter it but also to have it explained. As chance would have it, that it simply could not have been otherwise, in addition to playing a considerate man, he also had to bear responsibility for this tacticbecause of which he felt that he was suffering greatly. Hence the form was logic – he concluded, but its essence, indeed, was muddle.

The fact that he came to her did not mean in his mind that, actually, she did not come to him. It could very easily have happened that it would not turn into a quarrel to bloodshed almost every day. What did not get through to her, he could thank his own admission that her confrontation would ever more provoke him to clash even more with her. It was enough for him to establish that he stood quite firm in his convictions.

Thereupon, J.M. laughed calmly and briefly, staring at the stars.

You are an interesting character – Aman Fanny told him – gruff and at the same time melancholic. When you are in a manic phase, one can absolutely use you for their mental and intellectual hygiene, even pragma, and when you enter a depressive phase, the smartest thing to do is to leave you alone and to not bother you with any questions that a normal person would accept with gratitude and that would be indicative of attention rather than enviousness. You are then inclined to look at everything in reverse perspective. Simply put, pure paranoia! And how – you tell me – to unite a genius and a madman in what I intuitively feel to be the purpose of my life?

Aman Fanny's temples, which were covered with thin chestnut-colored hair, featured swollen veins.

- I like that jargon of yours, especially your manner of expression – he said. I expect it to change with the seasons.

What do you mean?

In winter and fall you will be a little shorter and in the warm season you will be a little longer, which suits me perfectly. When it's cold, I cannot stand long sentences.

Here, Aman Fanny could not restrain herself. She flew off the handle and started to quibble.

You seem to be defending yourself from something? he asked her.

I defend myself against insults and belittling. I had aversion to that even as a little girl.

Thank you very much, so I will apologize only because such high thoughts are far beyond me – J.M. said. I also find this conversation to be well beyond my horizon.

Aman Fanny was pursing her lips. J.M. was coughing lightly. Aman Fanny twisted her lower jaw. J.M. was sighing. He remarked politely: "It is apparent that there is a kind of generalization by which you give a personal color to objects. I have a feeling you might as well be killing around you."

And you are precisely doing it! –Aman Fanny warned him.

J.M. coldly admitted that he lacked the organ for this type of mysticism of death and killing and that he did not regret not having it. He enjoyed his utterance which, instantly, eliminated all difficulties and overcame almost all obstacles. This was evident in the fact that she was now surrounding him with a desired loneliness that put him in situations completely strange and dangerous to a man. It was also a sign that he was holding her directly to account and thus exposing his pedagogical anxiety.

Snapshot of a landscape of unborn tears

IT WAS VERY painful to have this hand close to him, restrained in the dark out of fear, decency, chastity, ineptness before the confusing demands of mind and body, but J.M. knew well that if he did not put his hand on Aman Fanny's shoulder, it could not be the victory of chastity or avoidance of violence, because love cannot be stifled, nor isrepressed love thus dead, so he fought with all his senses confusedly and feverishly. For this reason, he rebuked himself, though his lips were stiff so that he did not even try to use them. He felt as if some icy hand was grabbing him by the heart, and he realized that he was not entitled to big words, big gestures, or even stronger expressions, for he was the one provoking and he could only blame himself for all the inconveniences that had befallen him. Time was passing him by, in fact, for him now time did not even exist. A strange man he was, melancholic as much as natural.This self-deception, at the same time, was forgetting and believing, succumbing to stout-heartedness when the process was nearing its tragic end to the irresistible sleepiness that overwhelmed him like going around in circles when one wanders off. In such a hopeless situation, he had the habit of comparing his wistfulness to a deceptive and rosy outlook, only to give the impression that he was strong and healthy. In this way he comforted himself and hoped that his words, at least a little, would alleviate madam Aman Fanny's pain. Whether his luck would hold out was obviously a side matter for him, simply because he had not for a moment doubted it. This must have brought him some mental relief that caused him to even have unstoppable and hysterical attacks of contagious laughter, which must have enthralled Aman Fanny so much so that she herself began roaring with laughter.

She waslaid like figure eight through which she looked at him

SHE COULDN'T GO on without being impressed. J.M. felt comfortable in front of her precisely because of the words he had uttered earlier. He enjoyed the fact that her eyes were now resting on him. He dared not make a single grimace as a counterbalance to himself because of his own mental fear and frantic stiffness, so he hastily made the decision to just blink, hoping it would bring him a sense of relief. Besides, it was not clear to him why he continued to dream in such a mood – not in pictures any longer but in thoughts, yet in a way that was not less daring and offbeat. He still felt real remnants of his dream in his body, some icy chill in his heart still full of joy. He knew well and he well learned that decency and grace can be the best response to monstrosity and horror.

At that moment, J.M. started laughing, and she was smiling, though it made him quite worried because it was a cause for concern, so much so that it seemed odd to him. It could be said that he was observing her in the outer light, believing that he was noticing her in the depths of her eyesthat were vaguely widening, getting a deep, pensive and threatening expression in contrast to that firstinner light with whichthey radiated and which would be completely mischaracterized if one were to say that J.M. did not like it. On the contrary, he even liked it, except that it did make him a bit worried. In short, he was still undecided and unclear with these impressions for it was impossible to speak about them butunclearly, as such was their character.

Looking at him from the side, Aman Fanny couldn't get enough of him. Their shadows with predatorily extended claws were sliding, descending in the perspective of the street. It was clearly evident that the two of them were two giant spiders covered in cobweb. He tried to reach for the revolver at his thigh, but his fingers failed to obey, his nails were scratching at the leather of the holster without finding the button.

He turned with an effort. At the open door, eerily still, stood a flat cross, staring straight at him with piercing human eyes. He knew that this cross of boards wanted to do something terrible to him. Then, leaning against the wall and tensing all his muscles, with his feeble hand he reached at the slippery grip of the revolver and fired. But no shot was heard...

Aman Fanny took a cigarette, blushed, shoved it into her mouth, took a drag and started coughing. She was taking the air indeeply, and admired it whenever J.M. exhaled.

That moment she completely came out of his face. When J.M. looked at her, he saw her watching him from the mirror with dilated pupils behind her closed eyelids, which were entirely transparent. J.M. entered the mirror, clasped her tightly around the waist, and instantly began to break the sisterly tenderness of her resistance.

What is not to be given

IF A SNAKE senses you are scared, she will swallow you.And if she feels you are not afraid of her, she will take you to her gardens.

So, bestride the snake!

Aman Fanny chose the colorgreen because she did not want to die at this point; she totally shifted to disguise. This attitude of her corrosive sharpness shows how she threw down the gauntlet of disdain. Whatever. The issue remains sentimental and is associated with a certain mystique, so it should not be touched. I admit, though, that I do not share the acrimony of her certain critics when they touch upon these issues. After all, she was a woman who had no coldness in her eyes and who, at one stroke in those same eyes, cut her father in half, so she must have been as brave as ten men. Such fame followed her from the moment the word on this feat of hers got around. And right away, she became the darling of all men. But she was also a woman who got entangled in her own chimeras and who, claiming it to others, believed her own lie. The unfortunate thing is that she did not kill her father;when she closes her eyes and opens them again, she instantly dispels the delusion, and swallows such a deceit at the same time. Others did not allow certain things that were taboo to be messed with… She, who had always been able to laugh and make fun of the flaws of others, had a hard time accepting that her own were being brought to light. She kept on dreaming that she was alone at the top of the hill and crying her eyes out so that each of her tears could set the mill in motion…

She loved the truth and had the skill to detect a lie immediately, but also to recognize smoke screens. Incapable of diplomatic tactics and compromises. Hence, she was doomed to loneliness, for everyone was afraid of her. The air around her was so morally clean it was not for breathing. Whereto did Aman Franny disappear from the flames? It's not in the least easy for story heroes. But it's not easy with them either. Each of them in their own way crosses the boundaries determined by their family, possessions, past, offspring and, ultimately, by me as an observer.

Who is she? Is J.M. to accept her as a form, or just as a face, or as a soul? To understand her, he had to reach the line of peaks, pause at the horizon, hesitate among the clouds floating to the heights and coming back, and constantly describe that wave horizon in concentric circles, narrower and narrower, to his very being. And then it is only logical that this kind of environment takes him to confession, to soul-searching. But he will remain blind, he feels it, so I could say that he will be in a certain state caused by music and inner desolation.

Ah, who knows?

Ah, who knows anything anymore?

The constant residue of the night creates in him the impression of a void ready to swallow the inner events. She is his obsession, a space that separates the view from his world. Some force.

The sky at moments when the day is running out. A night the color of rusty copper. No sign of life. A city glimpsed in the depths of darkness seems deserted. She is more in tune with the landscape. She is convinced that *tout le monde*[1]covets to go to bed with her. Her imagination always stirred the tranquil surface of life. Her only problem was that she tried to persuade people she did not respect of her values.

He lacked many details to complete the image of her. He did not know, for example, if she wore dark stockings with seams under her long dress; he did not even have an idea of the shape of her leg - what it looked like below her knee pit, and what her ankles were like.

She as a whole arouses him with her richness, her contradictions, this natural disaster, which at the same time could be a product of the mind, thisunity of heterogeneous elementscalled – Aman Fanny.

There is no doubt that he is trying to find within her what to him had already been crystallized. But be that as it may, his look is neither innocent nor superficial. One may suspect that he knows the laws of the limitations of his love. Everything that comes to his mind seems to be weighing him down with the same forceful power as in the moments when he torments himself confronted with bare reality.

---

[1] *Fr. – the whole world*

He still doubts, he feels remorse, it seems to him that it was about something else. Nothing is simple, nothing happens naturally. Everything is full of stylistics and choreography.

Her gaze immersed in him. The color of eyes is cold, this time almost metallic. All elements, which remind him very much of the strict seriousness of the imagined person, seem to move in some of their inner space. These are his inner repeated problems with the troubled psyche. He is serious and melancholic. Everything he failed to accomplish in his life, he decided to forget.

Meanwhile, the heat had filled even the last millimeter of space. Heavy and dry heat swept across the hermetically sealed room. J.M. first took off his coat and threw it on the floor. A quarter of an hour later, he also removed his shirt and remained only in his pants, hairy and bony.

It could not be endured. Despite the unbearable heat, he felt a chill that came not from his spine but from somewhere in his consciousness as the memory of his mother. In a cold little church on the hill, he stands beside her, holding her skirt, and she is praying before candles, icons, cold basement cressets, in semi-darkness from which frozen dampness and cold arise. It is with that memory that the chill permeated him again and made him shudder all over. But when the intensity of memory subsided, just as abruptly as it had engulfed him, he felt the terrible heat dazing him and, localizing himself within it, realized that it was about a lie.

At this point J.M. truly flew off the handle.

Snapshot of a landscape ofjealousy over someone else's kisses

AMAN FANNY LOOKED confused and almost absent from that startled confusion.

Did she mind him destroying her?

His violet eyes were glowing brightly, calmly, pleasantly, perhaps even cheerfully. His face was serene, taut as ever. His hands were resting on the table. Fingers - thin, supple.

He cast a glance over Aman Fanny's face. He might have relented and kept listening to her, privately, but the pain held him back. He watched her innocently and intently, with a look that cruelly called upon him for devotedness and sincerity. And maybe he would have started with it, despite the jealousy that was stinging him as she was telling him about some distant bugger who had boned her on the office desk, and all those numerous folders had slid off its surface (filled with so many charts, tables, reports, studies), and all of that had landed on the floor because of her and for him to get in between her muscular thighs, but how and why and whence that cognizance came to him, he would not be able to explain, but then again, it was clear to him that the innocent charm of his face and the intent, calm gaze with which he was looking at Anđela was, in fact, just some complicated, cold, indifferent attention of the investigator who measures and examines the weight and content of every word of confession.

He doesn't trust her, and the thought of him not trusting her caught the breath of Aman Fanny, who persuaded herself within and within she flared up. And died down. Instantly.

It was strange, though, that neither that wrath, nor hatred, nor insult did hurt him.

She felt fear and hatred. And to avoid giving herself away, she went to the window, paused and looked outside.

She removed her forehead from the window glass. Everything she saw, she saw more from memory that was a flawed memory on the basis of what happened.

J.M. was sitting in an armchair, smiling gracefully, remaining silent. That grace was his armor. She discovered under that armor of patient calmness, equanimous concentration and gentle smile the wild, passionate, frothy, destructive power.

J.M. was still sitting motionless and his face at attention, but he obviously wasn't so calm under his skin.Someone in his own self gave him orders.

Aman Fanny was never quite clear about his gaze, which could not be forced into any of the well-known drawers, not even into the one with the "enigmatic gaze" label. And yet – he embarrassed her, confused her, disturbed her when he would look at her that way without feelings: just the ability of viewing objectively like a photographic plate, which is not judging but registering.

Aman Fanny shivered, but immediately overcame that quiver.

Snapshot of a landscape of a scandalous reflection and the parabola of the bounce into the unknown ± ∞

ONE MORNING I woke up as a woman. The underarm hair spread a smell of hair between a woman's legs. These scents were quite specific and well known to me from somewhere.

I pulled up the silk stockings and barely fit my boobs into the shirt. While I had them in my hands, they reminded me by their weight and shape of someone I know well.

In the bathroom, I stood in front of the mirror and surprisedly stared at my figure. It reminded me of someone, of some female figure.

I thought: people live in their minds as larvae. Only some turn into butterflies and leave the chrysalis.

As if I remembered something, I slipped my hand between my legs and felt her golden pussy there. I smiled with relief and placed myself before the mirror again.

From the glass, her face is looking at me. Everything suddenly became clear: I had turned into Aman Fanny.

Not only did she hand me down her face and boobs, of which there were as many as her arses, but also pledged me with and handed me down her supernatural beauty with those sad eyes that carried the constellation of Taurus within.

Dreamers have no homeland and dreams have no knowledge of a language. And Aman Fanny above Aman Fannies, what could it be but a dream?

My eyes alighted on hers in the glass like two black doves. The woman there had a chignon full of quail eggs. From looking through my dense thought, my gaze numbed and I decided to write a story about it.

What do stories talk about? About the wrong we have done to others, the wrong others have done to us, and the wrong we have done to ourselves.

But since the ink did not want to leave my feather, it will be written in felt pen dipped in a smile, in tears or in a kiss.

She burst into gigglesbetween her boobs, freckled like two goose eggs and abruptly cut her own laughter in, just like with a knife. I noticed that as soon as she got a bit excited, she would start making grammatical errors. It showed that her education was shallow, so shallow that she couldn't even wet her socks in it.

It was raining heavily outside in the dark and at the same time in my story. It was night in both rains.

All my life I have tried to get out of the role that was intended for me.

My smile, like a morsel, clung to the left half of my jaw.

October has never come as often as this year;every once in a while, and here it is again.

It was snowing heavily. As he would open his mouth, his tongue would be snow-covered. Only the sky would sometimes become blackened in a fast cloud of birds.

Beauty is a disease, I thought. A beautiful man is not for one person.

Her body had been deeply buried in his dream for some time now. She had a V-shaped wrinkle between her breasts, and the toes so slim and perfect that she could play the piano.

As soon as she started making love to him, she got eyes that were 2 meters and 10 centimeters deep and airy, and deeper than that nothing could be seen. She had two large flies under her eyebrows instead of her eyes. Her left eye is like Scylla, and the right like Charybdis – thought J.M., caught between Aman Fanny's eyes.

Whoever passes between them will survive. Her gaze leaves slashes like a whip. As if she were telling me, if you keep on staring, you will realize that through my eyes one can see way too deeply. You better put your sunglasses on!... Then deflower my lips, they're still virginal and waiting for you! J.M., love creates lovers, and not the other way around.

He watched how her beautiful buttocks voraciously chewed her panties. He had a feeling that her arsehole was like a ducat and constantly had to hold both her ears.

He was rolling her out like the dough beneath him. Whenever she wanted to get away, he turned her over for another screw thread.

With water, which he kept in his mouth all the time so he wouldn't speak, he washed his member and plunged it into her all the way to its root.

- Here's a leg for you! –he said.

Instantly, from below, he got a mighty slap, hot as a crepe with cheese.

He wanted to climb out the window and take off with happiness.

Aman Fanny did not feel pain, on the contrary. First, she washed off the makeup with light, short movements, and then turned the light off without changing her position. During this time, she murmured a prayer within herself:

O God, we know you were gentle
and that you gave Your heart for us...

Horrors, and the beasts with speckled lips and navels instead of eyes came at him. The two of them had long hair spread from under their armpits and tied on their chest to keep them warm at night. His own way and rhythm of living, apart from the others, he spent his days in complete solitude, shallow but impenetrable.

Silence will take you to God, voice will not, no matter how much you bust your chops shouting.

She fanned out her eyebrows like a peacock's train. Yawning was something like a fishy laughter. Her mouth opened wide inarticulately and that was all she had to say at that moment.

An anchored smile on her lips as cold and heavy as a padlock. It was so shallow that he almost stranded on the teeth.

- Big love takes time to mature, and a little is there in the blink of an eye – J.M. whispered to her ear, which was as deep as a snail, at the same time closing the other, which was as shallow as a shell.

- Ride me and watch for both of us–said Aman Fanny.

- I'll walk for both–J.M. said.

- Ride me once more!

And he did, carrying her, walk while being inside her, and she was looking at the path they were leaving behind. Thus, once again, those two loved each other so passionately that the stars in the sky whispered among themselves and gossiped them.

Finally, J.M. spurted into her, but this time into that shell of her ear: "My darling, you who are holding my body inside yourself, I am tired. Let it leave you and rest through and through."

- I have become your homeland –Aman Fanny told him, and you are still foreign countries to me.

He slipped his hand behind, into her dress. With a furrow so deep along her back that sweat can go down to her butt without wetting her dress and waistband.

After all, like all Christian women with Muslim eyes, she had the most golden of all golden pussies, identical to the one he had felt between his legs that morning.

So quietly, she joined him and signed his back with her boob, shoving one of her pink nipples into his ear. With her tongue that was capable of swapping the cherry pits inside her mouth, she glued both his eyelids to his eyes. He murmured something but did not wake up. He nestled up to her half-asleep. He was surprised and burnt by the hotness of her teeth in a kiss, but then his desire overpowered everything and he clung to her, put together both her boobs into his mouth, and drew from her breasts into his dream a drink that neither of them knew what it was.

While so joined, he well felt it running out of him and flowing into her and filling her.

And that was precisely what propelled them, just like the cart wheel sometimes propels a horse.

- Your boobs grow faster than your teeth –J.M. told her - and then you got beautiful lips: the upper sweet, and the lower bitter like almond.

When Aman Fanny woke up this morning, she saw her chamber full of dresses strewn across the floor. She recognized her dresses, which she had thrown off in a hurry last night, inside out, showing the lining...

The only thing she could not make up her mind about was whether it was a dream or whether she was truly doing it in her madness and reality...

At the same time, J.M. dreamed that grass was sprouting on his back, and the bed flipping over under him.This usually happened to him when he did not know when to fall asleep Mediterranean and when Bosnian. His doctors established that when he underwent sleep fluoroscopy.

He had Aman Fanny under him, whispering dirty words to her, now into a shell, now into a snail. With the words 'am I fucking you?', he would usually come and an icy shiver would pass through his body, and with the words 'you are, my precious!', she would come too. They had time neither to kiss nor to change positions.

But the baby was not coming. There were no children for them, though she was lying in the shape of a cross.

And then he heard some sound as if a sparrow was chirping or someone sucking a finger. At the same instant he spotted a cradle. It was a real cradle let down from somewhere to the corner of the terrace. Not remembering how it came to be there, at first J.M. thought that it was empty. But as soon as he came close, he saw an infant, nicely swaddled, lying and sucking its finger in its sleep.

Hearing the steps, the infant snapped awake, laughed and opened its eyes. J.M. noticed that the infant had the cataract in one eye. It raised its tiny head, and looked at him. As if something pierced J.M. under the breast when the infant pulled the finger out of its mouth and said quite articulately: "What are you looking at, you motherfucker, rock! You damn well knew hot to relishwhen you put your prick in!"

He woke up. An aged smile was thawing on his face.

Whoever heals oneself of self, shall perish, he remembered one sentence from a recently read book.

And J.M. thought: who knows what wind makes your mind work?

The mind runs late, and love makes haste.

- See, you know it yourself. I must not do that to my husband – she said.

- Love is life, and mind is death. Do not gamble with what God has given you as a gift. Only bread, clothes, shoes and hatred man is capable of consuming in large quantities. There is more love, wisdom and beauty in the world than we are able to use up –he said.

- Find yourself a match–she prattled. - You think you can dribble past life! What will we live on?

- We will skip our shadows and in doing so halt at the top of the bounce...

- The dearest of my life! –cried Aman Fanny.

- I need you like the belly needs a belly button! I need only you!

- Loving one woman is the same as being an artist with a gift for creating only one painting. And another thing: the Islamic "yes" is not necessarily the same as the Orthodox Christian "yes". Utter only the nouns for they are of God, and avoid the verbsfor they are of Satan–she warned him, blinking her lower eyelids downwards like a bird. In life, everything depends on two things: blood and death. Learn that life is not the cure for death the way death is the cure for life, and that each day of beauty in life is paid by each day of ugliness.

As he was listening to her, he realized that mandoes not age evenly, round the clock, but, sometimes, one would grow older more in three days than in one year. Where is that J.M. who used to be able to bite a strand of his own hair by turning his head quickly? The left-mouthed, who used to be able to bite his own ear off.

And then he assigned two tasks to himself:

1. switch night and day and for the first time start working during the day, and
2. imagine that everything he did not love up to that moment, he did love. Hence, he will side with his enemies and things will instantly be looking up for him.

There are women who cannot find their way around the home and whose home is constantly a mess. There are other ones who cannot find their way around their own soul and there is a mess. It should be tidied up in good time, as afterwards it will be late. Because in that afterwards any similarity between home and soul ceases.

Aman Fanny obviously didn't know that. In her soul, defeats and disorders began to reign. She started to stammer, and to talk unusually often and beautifully in her sleep. She became left-handed and claimed that the left-handed were those who had been beaten on the right hand in their previous life, or those who would put their hand in the fire for a friend in a future life.

Whenever he thought of Aman Fanny, J.M. would see her boobs swinging left and right, not up and down. That's how she walked in "them". He watched her then with his stallion eyes as though through the bottom of a beer bottle, choosing to hold water in his mouth so he wouldn't throw a remark at her.

Then he would pour himself a beer from the bottle and only then place his glass under. He would next take swigs of brandy from the glass, holding it by his teeth and not with his hand. That's why everyone older than him addressed him with "You".

He was drinking until he forgot which was his right ear and which his left.

The amount of fear is constant in the world. The last people will go crazy with fear. If I fear less, someone fears more. Fear is something like a common property. These are the clothes that people had to put on after the expulsion from Paradise, because they became cognizant of their nakedness before death...

The next morning, J.M. found himself in a huge house where Anđela lived with her husband. In fact, she had been dying with him for years. With his long tongue, he licked her eyes flooded with tears, took her by the hand, and did not deign to even look at her husband. That one, too, was no less agile in showing his contempt by asking, for the sake of his crossword puzzle, if he knew of a small lake in South Mongolia. The third letter is R, blank, and blank, and the sixth is N.

Aman Fanny's eyes were filling up with the lake, blurring both of them before her, one like air and blood for her, the other as if she saw him at the bottom of that South Mongolian lake.

J.M. left his wife, and she left her husband.

One erotic drawing, which won a Belgian artist the first prize at the international biennale competition in Rijeka, depicting a wanton couple at the top of their bounce, is a memory of this story, which I just told.

And now, the continuation…

CHAPTER TWO

Beautiful women, the love of a man

1.

I APPROACH THIS story when, perhaps, some things better be forgotten and put away. Besides, as someone has already said, writing or telling a story necessarily means – spoiling it. But all the same, I have made up my mind...

I am sitting here, and the night is cold, and I am writing, and I know all that, and it seems to me that everything I intend to write about here has happened in just a few moments, although I am fully aware that as much as I try to recount all this concisely, all this lasted much longer and more complicated. Therefore, it didn't cross my mind that the whole thing would be solved with this story. To do this at least partially, I must openly face it. It is still in front of me, and I still feel it very well: certain scents, horrible eyes, the faces I'm already running away from, so that I have to run away from them straight to some empty and terrible streets, but to the streets of some city strange and unknown to me, where other people had no faces at all, which was a sufficient sign that they would not forgive me.

What tormented me the most were the deaf, desperate and endless time, the dreary alternation of day and night along with the boring and gloomy rains that bring forth sorrowful disgust, and so the only consolation I have left is this white paper that now lies before me, indifferent to everything I want to confide and entrust to it, first of all, to atone for some of my feelings of guilt and shame.

True enough, I think about this too: how is it possible that I still have this will inside me to whisperingly confide when I have long since dispelled all illusions and, for that, felt even a bit proud. So, the thing starts to repeat itself, but –now –alreadyin the form of a parody, which I neither manage nor want to manage, but – on the contrary–it seems that I am becoming the head court jester. But even being face to face with this awful case, I will have to resume the work I started, just so I don’t go mad from the gathered lightnings at the bottom of my soul, in the deafness of time, and not on any account to say something important and clever. This, of course, does not coincide with some vague premonitions of mine that, after all, at least in part, some honorable thing might come out of all this. The only help in this may be given to me by the great hope that I will prevail over my heart in which but a trifle of impetus remained. As long as the lie does not surprise me in the moment of confession. This story should be the rebirth as a result of my pure loneliness. I enjoyed it so much that I did not want even dogs to accompany me. I only fear that all of a sudden everything vanishes and that someone reduces this wish of mine to a huge, unpleasant, profane game into which I want to draw them to participate with me. But I still insist that all of this would suddenly vanish, since together we would feel that we were all drifting senselessly. What else is left for me but to hope that I will succeed in fully openingthis shell of mine, and give in to happy amazement. How long am I going to revolve my life around this white unwritten piece of paper? Yes, I, Lili Melez–of the year of our Lord onethousandninehundredeightyseven, of the twenty-ninth day of December, began to transcribe from the Great Book of Nature; I am the one here writing from dictation at a large walnut desk.

I would like to be three again. That's what I thought this morning looking at myself in the mirror. I can't remember exactly who I thought of. Certainly not myself. I would like to look at everything with irony, including my own face. Indeed, it would not be a bad thing to be three again –nothing would be clear to me, I would be blessed– no matter that I would have to relive all those departures, deaths, misunderstandings, acquaintances and conversations, to read again all those bad books, to roll, while talking, my Rs like the French do, so I could say good morrrrning, and to me, so young, it seemed that I was saying it in an oddly likable manner.

There, I find myself trying to squeeze something out of myself. I'm afraid that in the end it will come out differently from what I initially imagined. Writing too has turned into a technique, no more emotions, no one screws one another for mutual satisfaction anymore but for proving their own power and vanity. Everything around us is one big bullshit, so I still only care about loners who no longer have any illusions. I must write about such ones and endure such stories. In this–I say–my own solitudehelps me.

That fall, when mother ended such life of her own free will, I shut myself in her room and stopped communicating with everyone. Of course, this excluded my sister Karmen, who had been and remained my only connection to the outside world.

I have not been able to sleep peacefully in years. I usually scrape two or three hours of interrupted sleep. I get up and walk around a completely dark flat. A bit of light gets through from the street. I listen to the old, faulty furniture creaking. House ghosts refuse to pass away. It seems I know nothing about myself. Nothing at all. This is an opportunity for me to try again. These few deficient data, which for years I've been writing on various forms (birth certificate, kindergarten, schools, college, registration of residence, identification card, party membership booklet and so on). An uninteresting and empty biography, and a family story, should be filled with details of exceptional destinies, and the common points found between uniformity and excitement as well as between boredom and an interesting event. I feel I'm already dead. Everything I do, until the hour of physical death, will be pure profit. I'll call them all by name. Father is staring at a dot high above our heads, mother, as always, simply does not hear me, brother is preoccupied with his rubber ball. The coast on which our family photograph was taken is far, and completely deserted. Water, as in the millennia past, is undercutting the coast.

I can no longer call Karmen. The voice calling her does not belong to me. The street, down which wehad taken our last walk together, was sinking into fog. I dropped her hand first, and then Adrijan's.She had a velvety, translucent skin and large milky breasts between which, in moments of fear and shame, I pushed my head. We slept in the same room then. At night, when it was sure that everyone had been asleep for a while, Karmen would get up, come up to the window and signal for someone waiting outside the house, hiding in a doorway, weighed down by longing andthe sultriness of summer nights. The unknown man would walk in quietly and sit on the bedwhere she was waiting for himreadily.

I would turn to the other side, towards the wall, and try to fall asleep.

I was yelling into the dead of night, under the neon lights, but no one responded. Now I know what I was staring at back then: I was watching the end of yet another unnecessary, impersonal, reasonless, empty set of deadened seconds, minutes and hours flowing into nothing...

The news of her death within our family, if I remember correctly, was received fairly indifferently.

And then, one evening (it must have been this hideous, sticky fog outside), father left home. He simply packed up and left.

For days I stared at his spacious, emptied closet. Sometimes, in moments of increased loneliness, I would hole up there for hours on end. I missed everything, most of all him. It wasn't until two winters later that I realized that my father would never return and that I might never see him again.

The time of everyday life and poorly conducted conversations came again. I used to sit and keep silent, unresponsive, although I felt sick now and then, as if tadpoles were hatching in my stomach.

That's when I first thought of writing a story about a bizarre, lesbian love.I could have talked about reality, though I didn't know what it was, about everything that was happening to me. It all seemed silly and so far, removed from the high demands of my grieving soul that, already then, was bleeding pretty much.

The family flat gradually became deserted. Mom still lived in the perfect tense. She didn't pay any attention to what was going on, as if nothing existed at that moment. Sometimes I would come to visit her in the room, I think once or twice a year, but I would soon realize that the two of us had long since had nothing to talk about.

I mentioned that I have not been able to sleep peacefully in years and that I usually scrape two or three hours of interrupted sleep. I dream, just before the morning, when the night is thickest, a fishing net full of severed human heads, with grimaces of indifference, looking at me with their half-open, water-washed eyes, and I have no idea what that is supposed to mean. Then, I wake up in a sweat and for a long time, disturbed bythatscene, I stare at the opaque darkness.

May God forgive me if the images, which might be similar to my life, are to be arranged by my imagination. I am happiest when I enjoy the moments, which I had but few, almost negligible. At that point, I usually fear that melancholy would afterwards come along, for me just as much of an evil as my unhappy soul. Whoever would put themselves in my shoes, I hope, would forgive me, which I - the way I am - do not allow myself to afford.

It seems to me that I am not so malicious, which, after all, will be confirmed by my blood that comes from the deepest layers of my malice; indeed, I am not so malicious, though the undiscerning and unruly ghosts blame me, my heart isstillgood, it yearns for the good and seeks that perfection in God, which–of course– I consider an illusion, which yet must constantly be incited, even if it encounters huge and ugly misunderstandings between me and the rest of the world.

I know my behavior makes me so disgusting. I would sometimes give anything for the possibility to completely erase from my life the way I acted, which embarrassed me a lot, and which, by the way, was completely contrary to my character.

Naturally, there were many circumstances that more often distanced me from others than brought me closer to them. This, clearly, impeded our understanding. And just then, only the bushes, woods, trees, plants, rocks did hear me. It seems to me that no one was as lonely as I was. To alleviate this, I have to brace myself. Thus, for me, no external, material world exists. Oh, as though I feel the weight of that world and the incurable resignation about it.

Here is another apparent proof that I alone spoil these few cheerful moments with my unbecoming reflections, in which my sensitivity and imagination continuously hurt me. Wherever I am –weather dreaming, walking or dipping my head between my knees –the terrible images always haunt me and prevent me from relaxing. It remains for me to hope that one fine day I will replace this head of mine with someone else's, to finally reach serenity after savage destruction. So, I would have been happiest had the demon not chosen my very soul for his residence. But I still hope that I do not have a strong enough desire to part with my life. I am driven by the inner feeling of still being able to do good deeds. I do not have the strength of Hercules to help Atlas in carrying this world, or to strive to do so in his place. I will, like Daedalus, thoughimprisoned in his labyrinth, find wings to carry me aloft... I shall find those wings.

One more night is about to end: on the other side of the window, I believe, the day will soon emerge, the pallor of daybreak will spread all over the sky. All around lies the land that gives no indication of having woken up yet, but only here and there will its omnifarious life start moving and making sounds.

To do something against fear, I sat down at the desk again and continued to write. It was still night, I felt immense fatigue, but the fear had completely dissipated, and with it the curiosity. Because of the fatigue, I must have felt nothing but indifference, though it was not much of a feeling. I wanted to forget all as soon as possible, and turn my back on everything. The wide bed with still fresh sheets under the thrown-back cover gave me the opportunity to do so.

At the same moment, I unwittingly looked back at that door; indeed, Adrijanhad came. His bright face, inundated with freckles, was now turned towards me, his mouth agape, half his tongue hanging out, and saliva dripping down his chin.

I am trapped by my own feeling that he needs me, and hence he is orbiting me like the moon. I am looking at his thick, saturated lips, listening to the creaking of the floor in the quiet flat. I feel the weight of my own body. How to get rid of reality for that deep and terrible abyss I feel underneath myself.

Through the open curtains, the full moon rays are flowing onto his shoulders, his full, twisted lips, behind which I can already see his rotten and crooked teeth. The room is in semi-darkness. I don't hear anything from the pounding of my own heart. Is it an apparition that will disappear as soon as I touch it? I feel like crying, so I hide my eyes to be swept over by what is really going to happen soon. I realize that I am millions of pieces of myself swirling like feathers all around and creating inextricable tangles, driftsand gloriously high glaciers inside myself. Well, apparently, that's me! I would cry if I knew I could be a torrent of sound that would without an echo go to the universe.

I suddenly pull myself up in bed, staring around with my bulging eyes, and confused by angry hissing, I lose my balance, even though I know thatI should keep my cool right now. I hold onto the hem of my nightgown, exposed and frightened.

And then, all of a sudden, steps and voices wake me up. I run to the door and slightly open it. The voices are coming from the other end of the house. Just the way I was afraid of. The magic of imagining the worst has come true. And now those steps in the shoes with galvanized tacks on soles are coming down the hall. I close the door and lean with my entire back against it. I have known this step all my life, and yet I am still standing with my mouth open and my pulse drumming all over and shaking my body. It turns me into a child again.

Yet, I lean even harder against the door. It's enough for him to push it and I'll instantly fall. I am scared, there is no mercy for me, I will be punished once again and no one will ever comfort me. Tears are flowing down my face; my nose is clogged and nothings is good. I am waiting for my half-brother on the other side of the door to decide in my name what my suffering will be today.

Knocking. Three faint nail raps on wood. The air is filled with his presence. The wound in the chest slowly opens. I am a being with a hole in myself. Through the glass eye I am looking into the darkness which is now complete and almost opaque. I finally know that I'm a tragically marked woman, without my own name and without my own dreams. What a terrible loneliness, coldness and silence I feel in myself, it seems to me that no such thing exists even in caves. It's enough for me to touch any single thing (a box of sugar, a teaspoon, a coffee-pot, a lit cigarette, a cup of hot tea, a dress button), and its iciness instantly burns me, causing such terrible pain within that sometimes makes me cry. On occasion, I feel somewhat better afterwards, but the suffering and trembling remain.

This is my dream, which can have a bad effect if dreamed over someone's beautiful shoulder, and then, it's sad to admit it: suffering and illness have altered my traits. I have no other solution butthe odious and desperate one – to plunge into writing and to die a little just because I had no one to talk to about it.

Everything Orhan did led to suicide. The way he ate, the way he drank, the way he moved. When he would hit me, it would not hurt.

A blow, and no pain. And then, the way he would not let me out of his sight.

Without him, my body would have been disgusting.

My longing is mostly brought about byremembering that I once, indeed, had a beautiful smile, which came from a sad arch of my lips, so that "the sweetest and most distorted smile" quivered on them, as Orhan used to say straight in my ear in moments of the infinite world of love. I still remember the button on his shirt and his Adam's apple, always cut after shaving, as in a slaughtered and cooled-off cock. He was teasing me, why I was sad, probably doubting his manhood, and I replied quite seriously that one always felt a bit of sadness after love.

- Are you not? –I asked him, and after a short pause he replied that he was not.

I had a good time, though we didn't understand each other.

I am a woman ruined.I would like to think of at least one thing I have not failed. Ithink that once I possessed the gift of having superficial and light-minded conversations with people whose affection I cared about. After some life setbacks, I lost some worthy accomplishments, one after another. As regards these defeats, I think that they finally determined and rounded off my biography. I do not believe in miracles, not even that my life is a miracle, it's a mere rotation of shit, urine and sperm, and we're something like litmus paper to, in that chemistry or physics (or whatever?), possiblyturn blue from pain and suffering, and turn red, possibly, from shame, if we at all know what that is and whether it is for eating, or maybe for drinking.

What poor devil keeps us from taking our own life?

Now I get to the incredible essence of my story. This is where my despair begins and ends. What my eyes saw, happened at the same time. However, I must pull myself together and make an effort to describe that for which, I believe, language is otherwise poor.

Adrijan, with his huge dick, started swooping down on me, mumbling. I heard his broken sighs, gimmeee!... gimmeee!... because of which I started to back off; brother, do you know that I'm your sister, I opened my mouth in horror. But Adrijan, like a dragon spewing fire from his mouth, fell on me, pressing me down with all his weight that felt like ablock of stone weighing a ton was placed on me, and anchored himself between my spread thighs.

What he could partially see between my legs, which I had automatically tried to draw up a moment earlier to ward him off, inflamed him so much so that his hand gripped my panties, yanked and tore them as if they were made of paper.

My rejection further fueled his lust until he roared, mumbled, and cried when I saw his decayed and crooked teeth again.

I accepted my sin as something congruous with me. In the bottom of my eyes, somewhere deep, I felt tiny pieces of death prickling. I know that facial expression of mine: the sad eyes of a Christian woman on a Jewish face were sickly and anguished.

Now I was lying under him, pantieless. Beneath him lay a kingdom, a rough and great lake. I closed my eyes not look at that scene.

I myself don't know what made the bigger shadow in my soul, whether that scary thing of my brother-idiot or the redness I felt all over me. I fled through valleys and hollows, ran through narrow passages, but I still felt the claws of the randy and freaky animal. I felt him putting that corn cob and shucking it in me. On top of that, he bit my shoulder. He panted and moaned and stammered over me. Mumbling, he swayed, falling and rising without end and rest.

With my head turned to the side, I lied calmly under him for a while as he uniformly pushed it in and out of me, and then, suddenly, I moved my entire body and roughly threw him off me. That cob of his popped out of me, ejecting sperm on the sheet in sharp jets. It seemed that it silently fizzled out, and I instantly smelled the odor of rotten fruit.

I opened the closet in which I kept belts for Adrijan's pants. I threw off my clothes and, crying, in a sort of hope, I started to angrily and relentlessly flog myself. After the tenth, twentieth lash(only dear God knows), I tried to hold back the crying. I knew there was no hope for me. I remembered what Orhan was saying about my eyebags, which made me even more loving and prettier.

- Li-li... mahrry me! I want a wi...wi-fe! This niiice... I want more!... Gimmeee!

Then I remembered that I once used to whisper in Orhan's ear: "When I sleep, I dream of you. When I wake up, I think of you."

I got up and left the room. In passing, I kicked the Pekingese in the muzzle. The puppy started yelpingin pain, but still followed me down the hall filled with family portraits among which the place of honor belonged to Orhan who, with a pained facial expression, in left profile, was wistfully looking at something in the distance.

I keep these memories locked up, but I am also something more. The restless conscience, but I am also more than that. When all the lights go out, I laugh in the dark and sniff alone like the dog sniffs its poop. Will I be able to close my eyes to have my fate carry me down the main current, down the rapids, through dammed-up waters, to wake up refreshed at a calm river mouth? And why didn't I run away from them as long as there was another place where I could live? I believe I was pushed into some crevice. My supplies of compassion are inexhaustible. I need to be needed by someone, even by Adrijan the way he is.

I am confused and addlebrained when there is no one who needs me.

My throat is drying up and my hands tremble slightly over a warm and soft skin. With bitter and hard lips, I search for a beautiful and luscious mouth. The fresh and penetrating scent of the cut wood, the saltish tears flowing to the lips, the strangely bluish, distant mountains. I cannot hold in the trembling of the bones in myself. Everything is making me burst into tears, like a child.

The dawn of Monday, from somewhere I hear the whistle of the locomotive. The deafening full throttle of the truck over the section of Chopin's étude, like black over the sky-blue. The foam on beer glasses, hardened like oakum, passes like time. A naked and lonely young girl with doe eyes in front of the mirror in love with the eternity of her body. In the coil of life, in which we are strangers, first myself and my life –like a magnet and iron filings, and then my life against others– like a ball and a wall.

The corner of the attic window outlines the clouds. The socks in the corner, the names of some months in the corner, up in the corner – a spider on a deathwatch. I, also in the corner, away from him, open my eyes.

The grinning smiles sprayed with the fixer describe the current trajectory by pendulum. The movement of the pointer on a scale foretells loss. I go into a meandering oblivion.

The wicker chairs, the busted recliner, the pencils in a cylindrical box, the stuffed eagle-owl with half its head in decay. The trite and badly played Saint-Saëns on the old record with the accompanying needle squeak. The pigeons cooing in the attic, the Dali monograph, the New Testament, the Collected Works of Andrić from the Sixty-fourth, purchased from an antique shop.

Grandma's Hoosier cabinet and dresser, a pestle in the mortar, a hole in the carpet under the stool, a jade dog on the shelf, a figurine of Homer on the shelf, a clock under the bed.

The cigarette butts in the liver pâté can, my father on a stool, a few thousand miles away from here, is listening to the transistor radio connected to batteries with a rubber band. Mother's smile on the tombstone.

The hackneyed roles, the talks about timeworn molds, we memorize our roles without prompting, the lit cigarette in the mouth, the zipper on the fly of a pair of pants, you don't believe your eyes that it precisely happens as the eyes see, so I think that someone from afar is telling you about it.

Why do you have to lose it right when you're drunk and shake just because the music is sobbing? The futile appeal to longingto feel that I suffer for something. When at last will that damn rain fall from me, to sense the damp scent of soil? So much metaphysics in us!

I also try to reverse things: to sing when I find myself in an empty bed in the morning, to sing about a verse for getting old and about the fear of starving in the street; it was indeed all true that illusions have always attracted believers more than the truth has. We have been the same for years, with the same habits and indigo.

A run-over cat on the road.

I live in a false Order that conceals Chaos, I wish for the rivers that I will never swim across, I watch them from the bridge, and they watch me. I read novels that I instantly forget. Ah, what a bogus orderof solitariness.

2.

FROM THE LETTERS she sent to her friend Marina Ramić, it could nicely be seen that she longed for her.

I am mostly alone and I do not complain, since three good buddies make this loneliness easier for me: you, this paper I'm writing on and one irrevocable decision that I do not want to talk about here because it's not been clearly shaped yet. It does not matter to me whether I will live, and – if God lets me now – how long I will live. For me, it has just become very important how much I care to exist as less as possible in the so-called reality world, to which I, thank God, turned my back pretty much. I relax only thanks to bleakness of the houses and the lake by which I live, dogs without pedigree, cats, books, abandoned places, the silence in the snowy nights when I allow my melancholy to get the better of me, some dense forests into which I ventured with fear as a little girl. I would like to stand there and listen to the crackling of pine needles under my feet.

Loneliness, insomnia, restlessness and a return to books – these have become my inevitable concentric life circles.

I wish that, long ago while I was still young, I went mad and experienced this gloomy life as a madwoman. This can only be achieved by true poets and true saints whom I often longed for, but to whom I never, except in my wishes, came close.

The rest of the human race is not worth mentioning except that people have always been strange to me, and they have always looked like neighboring trees in the woods, which stand forever next to each other and know absolutely nothing about each other.

What would it, apparently, mean, if I felt repulsion and disgust for a moment? Does it mean that I no longer have any illusions about myself or about others, and that I no longer regard myself as an honorable person, and does it at least have any sense of insignificant deception, which I have brought to the comedy of sublime feelings.

Pure, through and through scoundrel – there, that's me!

Then, let's put first things first, without whining and lingering, resplendent God, and the only question is, shall I endure to the end? Hence, it does not cross my mind that I might need to blush with shame because it is difficult to guess what will happen at the end of this confession and remain of me without it. In the book, as well as in life, unbelievable surprises occur. I allow such presumption to myself if the story gets me into a situation where at any moment I am, with a good heart and a bird brain, threatened to dive into horrors of the body and spirit, and mark the boundaries, outlines and ranges of those forces.

Without any feebleness, I have to face calling upon God, ready to bring you all to the abyss of the truth and to plunge into it. If I ignore what will happen to me at the bottom of that abyss, I believe that I will begin to see the contours of my former face. All I want is a hysterical passion to understand what sense of arrogance lies behind this act.

It seems to me that even now I cannot understand some terrible sounds. They still reside inside me.

I met two persons in myself, and from that point on, I've been trying to figure out what kind of relationshipthey had among themselves. Before I try to cool-headedly get close to them and before I realize with painful horror that one of them was obedient as if hypnotized, and that the only thing left to the other was to think about her, I really have to admit, now already, that this time it is about a certain pity for self, which again is very often inherent to natural-born criminals.

My disquiet will not be any lesser for that. Finally, why did I choose to lay a clean paper in front of me? Only for God to relieve me of feebleness, justification of circumstances and cynicism because of them, for which in the end, any good intention must be wasted and then destroyed. I would not want these words of mine to have such a fate.

I am becoming silent and bitter. My peevishness causes a sense of utter abandonment in me, but still not to the extent sufficient to make me desperate. I capriciously glide over the smooth surface, and despite my own persuasion through seductive words in endless nocturnal soliloquies, I remained very generous in the speculations about my upcoming future. I was riveted to one place without the opportunity to offer anything to myself except for certain threats, which really frightened me and made me agitated.

I bet I managed to finally figure it out and it had to be clear to me how I would soon have to lose this game with myself. My defense was no longer as passionate as it used to be, because I did not allow myself recklessness to deceive one obvious thing, that even today everything is possible, only to avoid that darkest of possibilities. Therefore, it had to seem both painful and sad at the same time.

So, even physically, I began to feel loneliness and forlornness, which deprived my hope of the meaning even more. It was enough to crack a tiny smile, just so out of curiosity, to see if incredible and unforeseen things would happen, but my God, I can only now understand that you have – long since – abandoned a wretched me.

I was a plain piece of furniture in this icy room, which expected to be torn down at any moment and taken to the junkyard!

For deeper, more delicate reasons, after I had been convinced that there was not a Living soul around, I again felt a quiescent anxiety. So, what if they even found me, that horrible thought was hanging out of my mouth. I would rarely dare to have the audacity and honestly respond to this truly direct challenge, and for some time I would not even express any desire, but somehow, in order to suppress my fear and get rid of the terrible coldness from my soul, I would again contort my lip until I felt with the utmost depression a certain weird, vague and glacial smile, which was far from relaxation. In fact, it was more of a creepy grinning and a restless coquetry.

Strangely enough, at night I managed to deal more easily with the growing number of apparitions. To be fair, I also felt unearthly anxious with them, but exhaustion from the day would often knock me down and finish me off, so God sent me sleep as salvation.

The day was different from the night and if I may allow myself to forebode, it would surely cost me my life in the end. In it, I could not deceive anyone - neither myself nor others, because the piles of details that night was deftly hiding from me would turn up in the day, offering themselves to my tormented conscience in an increasingly painful silence and unsightly form. Anyone could then, like a real intruder, march into my anxiety with such a thunderous shout, which was the exact opposite of apostolic silence that truly reigned around me, rendering me even more cursed. Nonetheless, I still resisted getting engulfed in memories, and for this reason I used to sit motionless for hours in the same place, usually with a knife or a razor blade in my lap, to defend myself against increasingly aggressive apparitions, although I still had the same feeling that I was gliding over the smooth surface of a lake or a river, or something? Stillness is all around me, and I continue rummaging through my own halted light. In the pocket, against my thigh, I feel the plane of the mirror, but I dare not look at myself. Finally, would I have the right to wonder if even its reflectiveness would not want to accept me there? The only thing left after this morbid gag is to congratulate myself on such a witty trickery.

Will the oxygen in this damned sealed room leave me too? It also seems to feel how I suffocate.

The day was, thus, a real torture. Every object attracted my attention and grotesquely offered itself to my dread, grinning with each of its features, which would return to its place when I felt its hardness under my fingers, and I would not refrain from crying that instant for not being crazy yet.

When I would try to close my eyes, at that same scheduled moment, those nocturnal creatures would have settled under my eyelids right away, and I would get up in silence as in a sleepers' dreams, and enraged and frenzied I would have driven them away through the cracks, I would have imagined in an instant that horrible comedy, directed for me by my fate. I would have tried to get rid of those jesters, then would have opened my eyes wide and nearly fainted.

That eyelid movement would have led me to my everyday life, which had to calm me down for a little while; however, I resolved to be extremely cautious.

It was a sign of my little revenge over the discarded scenes, which made me so insane that I was all bathed in sweat, listening to the fierce throbbing of my heart. I just had to wish for that revenge to last a little longer than an instant since it could not be inexorable and incessant.

Fervid confusion reigned in my head and just when I would manage to catch my breath, a certain new wave would have already begun to climb up against my body, and nothing else was there for me than to expect my new suffering, and – eventually – punishment. That moment of lucidity, however, was only a stripe of lightning that continued to illuminate my abyss.

I thought: you await death to finally strangle and deliver you, and even death does not want you, but only mocks you at close range, and scares you even more with its presence.

I think I'm not far from becoming a true madwoman. That would be worse than death itself.

In a foggy night, I walk aimlessly down the empty city streets. Thousands of characters mill around my semi-consciousness. All of them come together into a single one –undefined and vague. He has neither face nor name.

The rain boringly drizzles, in fact, needles my drowsy skin. It's not from drunkenness. But because before myself and others, I had to finally face the truth. After all, one must re-experience the horrors of the previous day. There are moments when it seems to me that I'm seeing or perhaps dreaming all this. I wish it were so! I try to comfort myself somewhat, but after only a few moments I almost let out a scream because of that. I would love to most unwaveringly walk down a deserted street, and somehow strengthen the rhythm of my sleep-walking strides.

So, I headed across the small-town square, which was unbearably empty with a dense rain curtain in the background. I thought, there was no one who would dissolve and distort me the way I would like it to be done, to become at least somewhat stronger thanks to that, even if that would break me into shadows, which I would move with my body to all four sides. I would like to get underway and move that much so as not to feel dizziness and nausea from this terrible effort. It would surely horrify me that I, that very moment I believed, would have felt the grimace twist my face. That physical pressure in the body leads me to fairly well maintain the reality as it had long since been offering itself to me and which I accept without hesitation, but which still keeps me anxious.

My eyes make an immense effort to keep me from complete distortion since I distorted and disintegrated everything around me so that I would maintain balance at least a little, and keep my memories only to myself.

Everything is meaningless, echoes in me. I've already learned that somewhere, that ditty, and it's not worth my while and waving it around like a flag. Am I at long last going to find out how much damned or, perhaps, elevated I am, if that is not one and the same?

Who knows, dear God, but you? I am so small and miniscule to understand it without my mind clouding up. I wish I could fly into the air exactly the way a bird flutters off.

I cannot experience such happiness. It's more likely that I will be pushed down the stairs one day, and that will be the whole and only story, or rather – an opera.

Had a one-time demon, spellbound and aggrieved, cruel and ready for anything, breezed into my soul?

Melancholy tears me apart and some indescribable and irresistible purple sorrow. Sorrow precisely has the colorpurple. The words reveal me completely, and they completely bare me in front of others. So then, what do they serve for if not, in the monotony of numerous meaningless and unnecessary days before us and behind us, for bringing us finally to the wall behind which we had constantly looked for shelter and thought that we had just found it.

The only thing I still feel is this monster breathing inside me. Besides that, I considerably feel silence. I know that I had irretrievably turned into a bat, which will no longer bite anyone and which will be pleased for having managed, with its tiny legs and wings, to fasten itself to a joist, mind you, in total darkness...

3.

IT WAS QUIET and gloomy, the hour of dusk when nothing happens. Not even an hour ago I was possessed by lustful thoughts. The pain of parting was beyond measure.

In short, by all accounts, she was entirely into herself, which only made her even more unattainable, alienated and mysterious. But time will have told that there have beenno finer nuances to that mysteriousness, and that she has not possessed some greater inner depth.

She too looked him straight in the eye with indiscreet curiosity, but she did not allow herself the liberty of uttering a single word. Her vulgar theatricality, which he could hardly notice in himself, began to drive him crazy, and that made him feel increasingly sick and then became unbearable. He thought he might end up in hysterics any minute. To avoid this, he began to pray within himself, briefly, a bit piously, a bit pathetically.

She gave an impression of being bored. Her crescent-shaped eyes exuded a certain sugary gaze, so one couldn't not know whether she used it to ironize at his expense or to pity him.

His, however, were bluish, with a wild glow, perhaps because of their depth and the moist pupils. His appearance seemed almost scandalous.

She approached him and, with her fingers, wiped the tears under his eyes.

Pale by nature, he was now even paler, paler than lime itself. In that paleness of a little coney, there was something impersonal. Everything he was doing seemed as if done in a dream. Shame and mortal fear blinded him so much that he was bathed in sweat. There was no way for him to calm his heart or hold back the grimace of pain that made his mouth twitch.

Everything was turning into prayer. The smile on her lips was still tight.

He was already so absent-minded as though he were on the other side of life.

Although she was scared, it did not prevent her from trying to color her actions with a certain amount of humor. She reiterated to him that his small cock wastruly just skin and hairs.

He squinted fromanguish; hence wrinkles appeared all around his eyes. She said that in a childish, affected and whorishly refined voice.

His nose felt the smell of her hole and sweaty panties.

At that moment, his mouth was half-open, such as in people suffering from nasal polyps. He saw before him the image of the dangling horse penis, heavy and heavenly. He envied him so much so that he squinted again from anguish and rancor, and those same wrinkles reappeared around his eyes.

Through the window, he caught a glimpse of a tiny bit of the moon above the endless high clouds, thin as a slice of watermelon, sinking behind, leaving unnoticed and defeated.

I think it's time to stop addressing him with "he" and finally introduce him by his real full name.

Orhan. OrhanMelez.

Orhanis a city child, he is educated and hence with a very developed sense of dignity and self-irony. First he theatrically asked himself aloud: "Who am I? I am one terrible delusion, my life has always been a terrible convention, terrible humor, terrible principles, terrible duties, terrible gentilities, terrible acting, a terrible smile. Everything about me is terrible." This confession reminded him of a monologue of one character in some tragedy. All attempts to remember which tragedy it was, remained futile.

The moment she approached him and slapped him with the palm of her hand, he instantly had an erection from intense excitement. It was as scandalous for him as if seeing his father's bare member or his mother's bare vulva.

Everyone was now offered what was their weak point.

Orhan was still kneeling on the floor, exhausted as though he had been with three women. As if he had just hit the ceiling in his life at that moment: everyday rush, hard life, disillusions and botherings, life's disappointments and increasing compromises, and her respect for his human dignity disappearing.

And he rightly asked himself: "Why am I so unhappy when I have always thought that I was alone in the world?"

In the tormented half-consciousness, the flashing red eyes of a bull appeared, then disappeared, he heard the cackling of the molested hens from somewhere, his bluish jaws in the mirror after shaving, the oak sleepers between the rails full of stains from grease and oil, the fumes of which stink of tar and pitch. He heard several frogs jumping and splashing in the water one after the other, and in his nostrils, he felt a faint smell of gasoline, smell of asphalt, or whatever it was?

The parallelism of rails. The smell of hay on the slopes of the mountains.

He turned to Lili. His look became vicious from pain. He was seized with rage that kills every hope and stifles every good will.

But as though she was expecting it, she pushed her chair towards him and ran out of the room. His contorted fingers clutched at the table. It could only now be seen that on his forefinger he had a ring with the death's head, making it clear that anyone could end up that way if they tried to make fun of him.

A gloomy, distorted half-smile turned his mouth into a Venetian galley. His jaw ached with suppressed laughter and his throat convulsed. He cracked his knuckles.

4.

I WOKE UP feeling anxious and irritated. To me, this is not at all unusual; as it has been happening to me since I was a little girl, or – I sometimes remember it quite clearly – right after someone's hands got hold of me as I was leaving my mother's womb. I could not, now, seek the deeply hidden secret of my soul's restlessness. I don't know why it had to rake through me when I had long since ceased to fear anything: poverty, insults, and even death would not in the least be interesting to me. I ascertained these things years ago, so they are beyond the shadow of any doubt. Hence my wondering: what else is that restlessness looking for in me?

I cautiously stuck out my toes into the cold air, then my lower legs, then my knees. When the soles touched it, the floor was pleasantly icy. I could catch a nasty pneumonia, it came to my mind. I hurriedly started tapping left and right to find my slippers. Still, despite everything I felt some relief despite everything, as if I had gotten rid of some burden during the night.

I remembered last night's dream. The most important thing, I thought, is to accept everything without unnecessarily analyzing and plunging into the essence of things, without perfection and fancifulness.

I dreamed of Orhan. He told me that in recent years he had felt a passionate desire to kiss me and that, knowing of this impossibility, he simply could not focus on anything else. At first, he thought - he said - that it was just his little quirky whim, which also seemed a bit disgusting to him. Then it became more and more important to him. He wanted to kiss me, he said, but it never came to fruition.

- What was I like? – I askedOrhan.

- You acted so that you kept us all at a decent distance. Everything you said was contrived to remind us how cold you were towards us.

- How else would I act when already then, I sensed that your moonstruck gaze had long since lost every bit of desire for my body, and even for my soul!

- You, fay, will be condemned to be taken through the city, flogged on the pillar of shame and branded three times: one mark on your forehead, and one on each cheek.

I was still under the impression of the dream. I inadvertently ran my fingers over the skin of my face.

I got up.

Outside, above the trees, some strange fog was hanging. The darkness was gradually receding, the dawn, not a bit white but with a certain blue-greyish glint, was smiling above the distant hills. The birds were still dozing, I had yet to hear them, or, really; did birds dream at all?

I was standing behind the curtain, huddled like those birds in treetops, thinking how nice it would be to remove myself from this place and fly up high, suddenly devoid of all weight, to ascend endlessly towards the dark blue sky, where I would not hear a single voice ever again.

So, I was standing, concealed, and waiting for something to happen with me, but – alas! – nothing happened.

Absolutely nothing.

I wished I could evaporate. It just had to be the day when everything I felt boiled down to a sense of defeat. I left the kitchen again, and went into our bedroom upstairs. I sat down and reread Orhan's note, analyzing each tittle of his handwriting, looking for any sign of indecision or a moment of anger that could have been changed.

I saw a corpse in front of me and immediately recognized myself. I put my head between my hands. The harrowing accent of his voice and his deep conviction of what he was telling me reached my ears. I could feel him spitting straight in my face, and that was why this immense hurt continued. That corpse sat on the floor, a foot or two from me, staring at me with the same astonished look that I had staring at him.

I went to another room and he followed me. I thought it was one of the dreams I had been dreaming these nights. I felt around myself: everything was tangible and in its place; nothing airy as in a real dream. That corpse, that is, I thought it was just me, sat down the moment I sat down, and at the same distance from me. I tried to caress him, but he dodged. He can no longer – I thought – live without me, but he doesn't let me touch him, he dodges instead. At that point, I really saw myself, or better still – recognized. Not as usual, though, not in the way I used to and that may have been true just because I got used to it. This corpse, his anatomy, this was me personally. So that's what I looked like. I was naive and took everything for granted. The corpse in front of me was saying something to me, moving his lips silently. Except in the mirror and in the water, I saw myself for the first time, but in the same way I could see my other parts, which, again, was – me.

I remained sitting with my head dipped between my hands in a state of complete paralyzed stillness, getting ready to make the journey to the center of the earth any minute, through the volcano's crater. I thought I would vomit when I pulled my head out of my hands. I got up, walked over to the table, and in one fell swoop I removed everything from it to lie down on its flat surface. For a long time, I lay on it, staring straight at the ceiling, forcing myself not to cry, though I felt tears fluttering at the edges of my eyes.

During those few minutes I was absolutely preoccupied with myself. I almost saw myself the way others saw me, but did not tell me about it. What I saw was the physical, material part of me. I wanted to make a move out of paralysis, but I couldn't. I remained lying on the flat table board and poked about her inner self. If it was me, surely there was something else, maybe the entire oceans of something else. Anything, anything was possible. I felt my heart beating and beating. In the meantime, I stretched out my foot, wiggling my toes at him as a sign of greeting. God is my witness that I tried, but I cannot love a monster, even if it were me.

With a long, composed look, I say goodbye to the sky and stars. Why all the magnificent sunsets, the crickets all night long, and birds at dawn and the floating dust particles? The image of the swallow diving, rising and traveling.

I'm yawning with boredom and then have fun pulling wings off flies.

Where are my feet taking me, and all the places they've been? Yet, on all these roads, I carried my native place in my thoughts, but with it also some imaginary piece of my lost world.

Through the window, the moon casts its light on the bare table. One plate and two cups are in the sink; waiting for someone to wash them. The carafe with coffee is still warm. The beauty of the world I live in takes my breath away.

Why can't we accept that our Lives are empty as well as the desert we live in, and why we can't spend our days cheerfully, counting sheep and washing dishes. I don't understand why the history of our lives should be interesting.

My shoe soles are uncomfortably sticking to the floor. I wander around the house without a plan and aimlessly, and leave traces that I will have to clean. I am the thought that crossed my father's mind many years ago. If only it would rain, everything would be easier, for smiling lips are not necessarily a sign of happiness. I need history and culture, hope and desire, moral sense and theology to be happy.

The cold wind whistles under the leaden sky. I'm getting old: skin atoms, mortar atoms, rust atoms are being forgotten. I turn my life into a fabrication out of sheer boredom.

Look, the purple soil around the mulberry tree from the fallen mulberries. This is because sadness is always purple.

We must believe in what our clocks and calendars tell us. Love messages from gentle blondes on the mirror, written in lipstick, melt like foam on the sands. Red and blue flowers on the summer shirt of a drowned man. A swan glides across the lake, a window blurred by someone's breath.

The circular saw screeching was coming from somewhere. In the avenue of linden trees and their scent, the street of washed August cubes. Beer foam runs over the pitcher rim. In lieu of flowers for funeral wreaths, the half-open door of the small chapel in the cemetery. The stroke of the cue on the billiard ball.

Embers glowing in the open furnace door. A torn piece of paper from a notebook, a kite sent into the sky on a tight string twitches in the gusts of wind. I can't go back;a life came into me that has already taken me. On the concrete slab of the tomb, an iron twigwith twofixedcollared doves.

Across the blue sky, at high altitude, a jet is flying. On the ground, anunsnuffed cigarette butt still smoking. The oakum of beer foam on the glass of a glass. The door handle is moving. The wall dampened and cracked from urination. I look at the books on library shelves as the conspirators.

The pot lid full of droplets of condensed steam. The flashing blue light on the roof of the ambulance. The insane buzzing of the swarm of blowflies on the warm-blood fresh ox's thigh. The sound of their wings and bodies weaved through the air a large and vibrant image made up of curves that move continuously as electrons move around the nucleus of an atom.

I'm standing barefoot on the cold kitchen floor. The city is dead as if it doesn't exist at all. The emptiness of the bathroom makes me quite sober. I know I will have a hard time falling asleep by morning.

The hand extended for a cup, the animals on the coats of arms climb heraldically. The girl with a mirror in her hand. Closed eyes between two rows of tall candles seem to be politely remembering something. Heartbeat rhythm on a cardiogram, with a trace on screen disappearing instantly.

A dead fly between the window panes. And then I remembered that solitude is an immense thing and that it is always bigger than our heart. I also remember the people I abandoned. How is it possible to abandon people?

Someone's child is crying in the neighborhood. Washed plates drying on a rack. The horse's tail flicking away tireless flies.

The officer on a rearing horse. The foam on the bare forearms, the white pearls in her ears, the silk on the edge of shoulders. The bubbling of the boiled-down jam.

How much mother wanted me to be a boy!

A lace bracelet falls off over the hand. The green-and-purple parrot on a perch in the cage. Some door opened. I saw no one at it. Mother was said to be a great lady.

A spring-lady.

Instead of being proud, I felt insulted.

The hand touches the stone pillar from which the iron bars rise. Why is it created when, one day, it will be dead again?

On the crucifix, down Christ's plaster ribs, the red color that should represent his blood. His inconsolable chin in the shadow of his cheeks and his head tilted forward. His mouth like the opening of a drainage pipe. Why do we always carefully pass before him? Because, I guess, I have neither his strength, nor his proportion, nor his velvety words, and also, I guess, because my voice is stuck somewhere between my throat and my heart. I am, therefore, a drooping doll with whom lifehas played more than its fill. He too must have some memories for sure.

The streets are still long and quiet. The day is breaking and the wind has subsided before dawn. It must be Sunday.

It's been long since my face beamed a smile, similar to the one radiating from the stone saints. The skin taut on the forehead and the back of the head.

Hands in silver washing dishes. There is always a sequence of their taking and existence. Is it possible to establish a connection between the spoon in your own hand and the steaming plate?

The orchard permeated with apple scents. The mouth with elongated, thin, lipsticked lips bites off overlarge pieces of apple and fill with them. At the bottom, the dregs of sweetness itself.

The light in my room is on for a long time. I don't always lean over the pages. I lean on my back. I close my eyes for a word that has been read many times, and its meaning circulates in my blood. Several multicolored buttons are rolling in the nightstand drawer. Outside, the rattling of a distant storm can be heard. In a movie, the gunfighter rides into the ranch with the burning sky in the background.

Relieving oneself in the outhouse behind a fig tree. Flies are buzzing intensely in the dark space. Tepid drops of rain begin to splash from the sky. In the air, the stench of excrement from below.

The sweat accumulating in the armpit, the insipid breath from the mouth, the stink of sweaty feet, the sharp stench of urine, the sultriness of the bedding of a grown-up girl. Silently and softly moved the shadows as if making love while standing. My grief is similar to dust and ashes.

A grimace of a smile, from afar. A tiny silky threat jutting out of tablecloth, the crumb falling off the table may break as if it were glass.

Is it truly possible to express in words a feeling of a man when he suddenly sees the sea? Something like lust on the breast of an imaginary mistress.

An apple on the table. The apple is red. How many lives orbit this fruit!One has always seen with the mouth, not with the eyes. I'm waiting for the gable of my birth house to finally appear.

We can still only go to sleep for free. I don't move through the world like a knife blade cutting through the wind.

The ash on the grate is cold. The particles of dust drowsily climb the sun rays. My knowledge smells of the press, it does not resonate with the human voice that tells the story. Further and further, I suppress the memories from myself as salty tears melt over the stone.

5.

I HAD BARELY gotten on the bus, and my eyes were already running over the seated passengers in search of a vacant seat, on which, so tired, I would happily tumble downwith a whole pile of books in my arms. Since getting to my stop was going to take forever, I had to find a neat way to sit in someone's vacated seat without hesitation, whether or not someone was more entitled if, by any chance, was closer to it. I can safely say how in such mood I was determined to accomplish that, though I was not quite sure that I would really have done it if a similar opportunity had presented itself to me.

As I said, I wasdead tired, since I had spent all day at the college, as it were, with no breakfast and lunch, save two sucked-on candies, so already then, in my mind I was creating a 'what to start with' strategy upon opening the fridge. After all, I never really cared about having sweets before salties, or vice versa, especially now when I was hungry like a wolf. I thus caught myself chewing on my own tongue.

I have neither time nor desire to discuss how I myself supported the theory that humans, by their nature, could very easily all be cannibals, so if one would find oneself in the throes of things, one could peacefully bite into one's own flesh. That's how I was throwing balls about in my noggin and all sorts of such silly ideas, completely desperate in realizing that we had passed only one stop.

The bus was full of passengers. It seemed to me that all those people had vowed to travel just when I did, but to make things even nicer, using that same bus that I was on. It was with genuine jealousy that, through the glass, I kept my eyes on a half-empty bus, wishing I could run and get on it, even though it was moving in the opposite direction. That detail made me think about it more thoroughly. Sometimes it seemed to me, in a frightening way, that I did not actually notice what was going on around me during the day, so I was impelled by this fact itself to assume that there was a terrible indifference in me for all that was happening around me. That's what I had thought, at least until then.

I cannot but mention here that, despite my load of books and the fatigue of today, I felt some enjoyment as I held on to the handrail like a monkey. It also inspired certain confidence in myself. Sometimes I would simply have a fleeting glance at the passengers.

Just as I was enjoying myself, I could see through a bedewed glass that it was raining. For a while, absently smiling, I watched the people under umbrellas. At times, I would find with a touching certainty that something like this was quite impudent on my part, though I have always maintained that the most ordinary wistfulness can often be hidden behind impudence.

Those outside were whisking by along the window I was facing. My recent taste was something I would rather more closely call cheerfulness. However, its consequence was that I myself made use of an artifice to convince myself that I was indeed a confused guy, who truly was worthy of a certain moral respect, but with the fact that he viewed himself through the others' eyes as his own, which represented what I thought to be terrible for me.

I would like to know if hidden in there is a certain delusive insolence that all conceited people have. How much, in fact, my way of shaking with muffled laughter or judging things through gushing tears is justified, I leave to my own discretion and honor. As far as I am concerned, I will continue to observe things like this either through laughter or through pity.

I cannot be certain that I was thinking of something similar at the moment the bus stopped at one of the en route stops, but I know for sure that chance would have it that across from me, two rows further, I suddenly saw a beautiful Old-Slavic head, which instantly not only caused me tremendous joy that made my chest flutter but also rendered me simply unable to take my eyes off of her pleasant, I dare say, heavenly appearance. The duskiness of her complexion, the blackness of her hair, and her calm and kind eyes might have led one to think she belonged to ancient Egyptian women like Nefertiti, if it weren't for the slight anger that she exhibited from time to time towards a young guy next to her. A rather short oval shaped her face, with an almost pointed chin, a nose not quite straight, slightly depressed, somewhat turned-up, and a still mouth (except when she would scold the young guy), well-cut to be neither sensuous nor sharp.The hair, which covered her ears halfway, was firmly pulled tight, so that the white parting above her forehead was shiny and undisguised. In spite of this, certainly not intentionally, tiny loose strands here and there were hanging very charmingly over her ears.

Her dark-skinned hands, neither too rough nor too well-cared-for, with a wedding ring on her right hand, had something so human and reliable about them that I felt immense pleasure in having seen them as well as her stupendous and not to small sculpted legs and feet in comfortable flat-heeled shoes and with red woolen socks, tightened around her well-shaped ankles.

Everything was – I dare say it – divinely pleasing to my eyes and my spirit.

I do not think I would dwell on the further description of what my eyes were watching at that moment, but I would dare say that before such an appearance I was blown to bits, already feeling the immense burden of those books in my arms, so I was forced to lay them down on the floor, under one seat, then put my foot on them so they wouldn't scatter all over the bus. But now I didn't pay much attention to them; I was looking at an unknown woman in front of me, and I realized what a blessing that handrail I frantically held on to was.

Here, however, I am forced to mention the following. It seems justified to ascertain that my mental distress at her extraordinary appearance had something of a telepathic touch, so that at one point, even directly, she looked back at me, raising those two gorgeous almonds of hers, and I, like any other typical fool, double-quick, looked down, so that the ace would not by any chance lose his balance because of it. Just in case, I prevented an accident.

When I looked at her again, she was already in a position in which I had been watching her before. I still find myself in a state of excitement when I think of her gaze, which I cannot interpret otherwise than a pure coincidence.

Like hell coincidence! Of all the people on the bus, why did she have to take a look at me? Is it because I was standing face to face with her?

I dare not believe such frivolity, because there was at least a dozen of us either sitting or standing across from her. After all, I believe that many things are colored by mysticism.

It was not clear to me that, guided by the charms of an unknown woman, I was back in my mind to things that had tormented me a bit before: right now, I am searching and waiting for the opportunity to have her look at me again, to once more see those two gorgeous almonds reminiscent of the gates of heaven.I'm stalling and beating around the bush. Someone's pulling me by the sleeve, mentioning some books.

Why would I need them now, and what do I care for some and someone's books? I have a duty and a task that drive me somewhere. I am astounded and afraid of that task. I'm starting to get scared of what is coming. I'm stalling and beating around the bush. I'm fully aware that my soul has burdened me for eternity. I am reluctant to attribute any tragedy to this chance encounter.I can't free myself from the dull anger of having been in the presence of this feast and fireworks for the eyes and the soul.

I'm starting to get scared. Should I enjoy this gift of God a bit longer, or should I already be anxious since the bus will soon reach her stop where she will get off and disappear forever.

By now I knew, and it was quite clear to me that she was obviously coming from the heart, which seemed, not only to me but also to my heart, as a somewhat surprisingly painful flash of lightning.

I will have found out later through my channels that this beautiful woman's name was Aman Fanny.

Onanists as the tantaluses of love

A fertilized seed of lovelater contradicts love as a mystery by virtue of invalidating this secret. That moment should not have outlived itself if, subsequently, it had not succeeded in renewing itself as a myth. Only in this way will the consistent misconception somewhat fulfill the requirements of the spirit, which, in and of itself, is problematic or paradoxical.

Why does man so much love, respect and care for his own love seed, while on the other side that same biochemical substance suffers, dies of hunger, is humiliated, and he – some less and some more – shows the utmost expression of absolute indifference?Does such his equality mean at the same time also his consent to destruction or to devaluation of that same existence, or does it deny all meaning of such existence? If both these points – indifference and denial – come into play, then the paradox of spirit opens up everywhere and is quite contrary to the spirit of temperance (something similar to how we treat children, poets and beggars – pathetically and fictitiously) just enough to renew in ourselves the illusion of how well we have learned our homework in humanity and sentimentality. Therefore, the occasional "sacrifice" of such spirit is most often the prolonged infantilism and proof of one's own powerlessness of love. He will look for his alibi for the absence of that love in his "banal family drama", while indifference or denial in the air will remain suspended in history as "the malice of the world", and the said alibi in the syntagma "archaic demography".

In fear of loneliness, and also being apprehensive of close experiences with others, which – of course – imply a great amount of intimacy, we meet with an extraordinary sense of emptiness, isolation and immateriality of ourselves, all of which will take place under intense pressure of remorse and constant fear of own transgression. Between this effort towards honesty and the sense that all of this is natural, the problem lies in how faithful I will remain to the language, or how I can use it to express some seemingly inexpressible things. Should I fail in doing this, chaos will engross my stars and speak of their light. So, there is a light reaching us and the perception of which I would like to share with others, which is utterly unappeasable if my shame and remorse are a rebellion against such words. Eventual despair will make sure that the question of my hypocrisy comes to life in me, for which I can lightly find an alibi that, for me, the illusions, which will delude physiology, are more important than the experiences that, before a witness, could push me into any action, with a dubious outcome and without a clear goal on top of that. As it is, everything stays between us: I took refuge in illusion. What I do, even if – say – immoral (in the biblical sense of the word) gets covered in delusions of this experience. Thus, the seed of mister Onan avoids the experience in its archetype, and avoids a living and life-giving relationship between the rational and the irrational. He may or may not (which depends), much like coitus, become a spirit of violence both over the body and over the soul, except that with the former I am a kind of double ruffian and reprobate, and with the latter a medical case and a wretch. As a ruffian, I try to reconcile two worlds between which both body and soul have dug quite a chasm. Such fictitious approach to this problem inevitably invites the language, which would like begin to speak of failure and expendability, if not categorical, then at least equivocal. Such dramatic lyricism puts this thing in a somewhat inferior position to be despised by those in whose veins runs the "blood" of life and who have not yet given up the good old bodily touch. All these tragic-pathetic gestures once again confirm the inner high and low tides of our sensibilities, cries for them, as well as the disdain for these sensibilities that goes to the very self-disgust.

6.

LET ME, AS a doleful dreamer and sad loner, be allowed to, all divinely blessed and aglow, continue this text – at least I so imagine – and I believe that it will keep leading me through tears and painful tension, which will neither add to nor take away from values and splendor for having once had a cheerful smile conceal the world of suffering, common contempt and rejection. It's a secret that with less and less hope I have intended to penetrate for years, and revive it through the foggy images behind pressed eyelids, but it seems to be too much of a duty burden upon me, which makes this secret even more touching. I, therefore, often feel a heart that is there to satisfy some form but not an objective spirit, which would unburden my conscience. So – I think that's what I decided – I abide by its commands, even if they are unacceptable to me and my moods. I cannot imagine it at all until – I and the facts, on the one hand, and I and my apparition, on the other– merge and synchronize in a harmonious whole, more or lesslike a key and a lock. Then all I have to do is to open my restrained eyes and feel if, with that painful longing, I have strengthened my inner peace, which has become the main reason why I began with this story in the first place.

So, I am in between my own reproach and sadness, in the extremely noble mood of the lost world called the past and the psychology of man who follows his own needs, desires and demands to revive it by any means and renew in oneself the pain of defeat, for I already, right now, appear as that distant past that will have to endure and suffer again to cope with my own love.

For a moment it looks to me that, the way I am, I really do not live in this world, and that this function, instead of me-the-apparition, is performed by someone else who manipulates me, and who belongs to that past. At that time, I hear his voice out of my mouth. The moon wandering across the sky I watch with his eyes and wonder how I, who once did not exist at all, can see all this, hear – alas, how much insolence, maybe even pathos! – and want to say something, but still I am comforted by the thought that, after all, it is not about me, but about the one I have been for some time – it seems – recognizing, and have exposed this very spicy plot. It was then I first realized how that spirit of someone else in me was not a stranger (or have I – unknowingly – adapted to it), but over time he became so alluring that it seemed that he had to bridle and restrain me a little, even admonish me, not to do for him what already seemed a bit forced on my part. Thus, it happened that I would suddenly become overcome by a strong feeling that I, in fact, do not keep some big secret within. That feeling must have provoked in my roommate the sense of realization that I had become aware of his presence, indicating to him that he was not to exaggerate with the revival of memories, since my potential death would be the reason for his potential end. Of course, we had to take good care of how we were to put each other to death and bring each other to life. All this had to unite us even more. I already felt pretty much like a bird flying and being able to recognize its flock for the first time. I knew by the constellation that I was right, but when I will reach it, only dear God knows...

The mission of the word is a sense of shame that will dry at least one tear, even if that mission takes place in a trash society. The words are a fragment of the sky in the corner of the window, the immature age of dreaming, like the cold touch of scissors. They close the extinguished eyes of a dying person, which, only a moment or two earlier, had been open and directed towards the endless sky's blueness. They hold an intimation of the chirping of sparrows and cooing of pigeons in the windows, a frame of the basket with fresh laundry. What words to find when before the half-extinguished eyes, in the corners of which glimmer the last bits of light, pop up the wide-apart legs of a tired woman and the jelly thighs are revealed? Then, usually, from somewhere emerges a threatening finger of the prosecutor seeking the death penalty for the accused.

The three-fingered hand of the lumberjack lies on a stained, checkered tablecloth in the village tavern. Has wistfulness nestled within him owing to the overshadowed retouch of the soldier from youth, hollering and rushing to death, thinking that he was merely an augury of death?

Everything with him is in the ultimate arrhythmia – his birth, and spirit, and genes, and climate; plain metaphysics! – while the outside was seemingly fine, so much so as to hide the secret of evil. He must preserve the unity of life and the unity of longing, to prevent dissipation into a thousand partial lives of petty longing and longing pettily, because only the longing of the eye, the longing of the spirit, and the longing of the hands are insufficient if no longing of the heart and the longing of thought exist. Only he was given the gift of overcoming the blurred and hopeless blindness. The tear only in pain becomes that which sees.

If only I knew how much going to bed for love is also going to bed in the name of death. (Only man knows whether precisely the Mother of God or our mother is that heavily made-up harlot with a blond wig aslant on her head.) By no means, it is not his deception but his divine destiny, that which is directed towards the path of his rebirth – the moment of conversion into God. In doing so, he will have to disgorge his final scorn and sin.

Unbearably harsh light penetrates the closed eyelids bitingly, forcing them to part hesitantly and sullenly, and then, soon, open wide with horror. By then time has begun hanging by a thread.

At the end of the daily chopping, the axe stuck in the log causes a sense of painful pity in him, as well as the agonizing and intolerable responsibility for what he would like to do – to cut in two the shell of oblivion with a piece of razor blade, and enter the realm of remembrance.

7.

I USUALLY WRITE so little that neither facts nor thoughts come under my pen immediately, so the writing of this story is a very painful thing for me. I am a lonely soul, almost without an acquaintance, hence I have no obligations. If I look around, I find neither to the right nor to the left, nor in front of me, nor behind me any social foundations that would lead me to real obligations. I don't know if it happened because they were sharply cut off, so now I felt cold indifference. Thus, I got to the point of living a completely negative life. However, the fact remains that I care to disclose my past, to talk about a little girl of seven whom they were raising as completely godless and who suddenly felt the compulsory need to pray, though she herself wanted to resist it, finding it contradictory to her knowledge. I used to masturbate daily before bedtime. The pussy seemed to see him sitting with his legs contorted, with that slightly bewildered and gentle expression that dog eyes have, and how his gaze was wandering, somewhere far away. To me, it seemed at the same time miserable and alarming and comical and, ultimately, soothing. His surprised, tearful gaze kept on wandering. He had unshaven cheeks with thick, black bristles, which shot up as in pigs, so he could easily scrub the floor with them. He was completely naked (I just don't know why I left the black socks on his feet).

The position of his sergeant was of such incomprehensible hotness for my curious pussy that I was no longer able to behave normally, so I smuttily asked him to do it as soon and as wildly as possible.

Since I found him in such position, one can imagine what a transformation occurred when his general stiffened, perhaps to salute, but a moment later, it collapsed between his legs like a frightened sprite. None of my fantasies could have erected it anymore. Then I felt a strange fear about it. I knelt by my little bed and began reciting a prayer:

Dear God, I lay me down to sleep,
Send an angel watch to keep.
And, Father, let your loving eye
Look down upon me from the sky.
If wrong I've done within the day,
Overlook it, God, I pray.
Father, guide me patiently
And may my faults forgiven be.
May all persons great and small
Feel your protection overall.

Although fate was driving me to write, I still did not want to do it, even though I knew that I would have to tackle it most seriously one day, not so much from aesthetic as from diabolical motives. Later, everything I wanted to do, and haven't done out of fear, perhaps out of shame, perhaps even out of haughtiness, I do and will do to my characters. So, I think I had an interesting life. That would be the answer to those who wondered why I was, for the most part, cheerful in life. I shed light on my darkness and made a great deal of cleaning in my solitude, which, again, used treacherous means to leave me even more stripped bare in my memory: here I am, in the morning haze, across the river, you can easily find me, of course, if you do not stray in the fog. Then I too am a tad confused by the silence, which is the only certain thing and will be the only one remaining in the end. Time will disappear, and it will remain. It's going to be a wild excitement that even now I feel like I'm standing at the door of my memories and my heart is pounding wildly in my chest like a door-knocker. I perceive the outlines of the figures detaching from the darkness, someone's footsteps echoing through deserted squares and quiet little streets. Will I be able to revive at least a fraction of a broken, mislaid oblivion? Will the morning, and the light, and the dawn ever come again?...

The scent of the fall spreads through the city, the golden and flaming colors floatacross the morning indigo-like sky, human skin smells like salt. It is with pain that I apprehend the fragility of our being in this city that sleeps like an antediluvian animal.

Perhaps memories will bring us comfort and salvation?

On the way back from the funeral, a neighbor asked me:

- And why did mother kill herself?

I turned a deaf ear to this painful question.

Ever since mother killed herself, I have heard this agonizing question several times: it was asked by my neighbor at the home door, then by those who received the notice on the passing, then by reporters who had not even seen Maman. Each time my conscience would be shaken a little and encourage me to write in a letter to my father: "Just tell me you killed her!"

The neighbor handed me a newspaper out of her pocket. At the pointed spot, I read that Aman Fanny, isolated from her family, killed herself due to neurasthenia.

I folded the newspaper and returned it. I learned from the same neighbor that certain other newspapers attributed this suicide to the sudden onset of insanity.

8.

THE SAME NIGHT I dreamt of going for the first time to Paris. I said to myself: it will be a journey to the stars. As I was in the role of asking, of course I appeared confused and humble, but this was no reason not to find with each passing moment how close he was to me, perhaps never closer. I heard his hoarse and swallowed*wi, wi, wi* (oui, oui, oui)...

I felt him staring at me from somewhere, and all that, somehow, was wondrously stupefying me. I was anything but indifferent. I felt like I was about to touch the skin of a man.

I dreamt, next, of Paris fleeing in front of our train. It seemed to me that we would never catch up with it. Suddenly I saw it taking along people, houses, trees, the Seine, the sky, the half-blind old barrel-organ players. Our train stopped, and so did Paris in its devouring. Our train moved just a little, and itshuge, antediluvian mouth moved just a little. Oh, look, a miracle: my Paris suddenly turned into a huge funnel so that the whole sky over Paris could fit into it and flow down. The funnel began to turn downwards; indeed, there was a serious danger that everything would collapse into it and fall through it like the last grains of sand in the hourglass. Some unhealthy, insane mechanism vibrated in me. I thought: I'm cold because I'm so far away from him.

I had burst into tears a moment before I surfaced from the dream for, I interpreted that Paris was, in fact, my unhappy maman.

Many years after that dream, in one of Haertling's stories, I found this: "When a man is happy, he gets cold." (The latter sounds too corny. First because I am not sure if I had really cried, and second because a few years later, this Paris truly savagely slapped me so I would not cry for it, not even in my dreams.

Curtained windows. The stench of the fishing port. Shouts and screams along the long shady platforms. Crowd. The smell of bolted upholstery in a train car.

On the macadam road, a village funeral. The wedding guests stop the clamor to let it pass between them.

The wide belt under father's suit. Mother's pleather bag, fake jewelry around her neck, a tiny wristwatch that brother gave her for her birthday, though it had long been father's promise when she was still a girl before marriage. The retouched photograph of them above their double bed.

The drinking fountain wall, on the road, all green with moss. First experience with a girl with glasses. A urinated-upon wall in someone's hallway.

The sky was as white as clay. There was no sun.

On the wall, a sliding shadow of the bird flying by. The sound of footsteps on a gravel path in the park. A moment when the phosphorus ignites on a match.

Above, the stars were flickering...

A snake, perched on marble, in the silence of the square. The window pane between the rain and the curtain. The eyes of the sorrel-coloredhorse at a gallop. Sailboats in the early evening.

A slain sailor on the bar floor. A glass of rum on the table.

Rain drops on the windshield of the one who returns to his wife from the still warm bed of his mistress. A shriveled carnation in the tuxedo lapel.

Water on the stone from a sea urchin taken out.

The killer in lacquered shoes and a deep-blue suit, with a baby, lily smile smokes a lot. He has a hawk nose and shoots right away. A smoking gun and readiness to go out and disappear at any moment.

Snow on the red rubber boots of a child crying for his mother because she does not respond. Breath fogs the window, a heart drawn in the fog pierced with an arrow. Closed eyelids on marble torso.

A dampened gauze is steaming between hot iron and legs of men's trousers. A young couple is expecting their second child as early as this week. Both misplaced their first loves.

My father, tired and gloomy, comes back from work on a blue city bus. His seed, once dispersed, filled me with every possible flaw.

Mom dies alone in the room. Billions of stars behold that quenched firefly. Bubbles of stagnant water in a glass on the glass of which father sharpens his razor blades. Anger, rage, sleeping pills. Disease in Latin in a hospital record.

How do I get out of this life the same way I entered it?

The befouled bronze head of the horseman by countless careless pigeons.

A wounded bird allures the vulture. Silent lovemaking with body sweating and subdued panting in anticipation of the final thrust, distortion of the lips as if it were a terrible pain and the invigorating serenity in the end.

In jealous consciousness, the body of the loved one over another woman.

In a photograph, a fat lady in the knitted cape, sitting in the lounger and sunbathing in the snow, with her head thrown back to the sky. Next to her, the skis, pinned into the snow and crossed.

Down of the fledgling in the nest. Blessed faces in public urinals. With tears in her eyes, the girl in front of the mirror looks at her wide-set and puny breasts. Zweig shot himself for the tragedy of civilization. For her, these breasts, like two sunny-side up eggs, are the tragedy of all tragedies.

A few matches in the open box. The snipping sound of scissors in the barber's hand. Elderly profile in a rocking chair.

Lovers would like to cover up the crime.

Youngsters would like an iced drink.

The roof tile is just about to fall.

The disloyalty of best friends. The ground floor window through which every passerby can see what's going on inside. A greasy smudge on the overcoat at thigh level. The inside of the smuggler's jacket.

The flank of a woman after love a man would like to leave. Above them, a book with the printed experiences of sex.

That woman should only once more be his before he decides to leave her forever.

Standing up, a glass of wine drunk in delight. The lower part of the pastor's robe follows in his footsteps.

Silence in the cemetery, in the museum, in the library, in nature with the occasional coating of cars from a nearby road.

The white pinscher with a black spot on the left ear and tail.

The goalkeeper's dream to wall in his goal of which even the wind will bounce off.

Tiny paper flags in the hands of children thronging on the sidewalks between concerned teachers and police officers. After everything, they haven't seen anyone, only the cobalt-blue light on the line of black limousines.

Scores overflowing with notes and discreet lighting on the stands.

Hard words of rebuke of ex-lovers. Only these words are in circulation: "I'm leaving!" and "Stay", or "Go, who is holding you back?" Everything is crumbling as in the biblical Revelation.

The turning of a fake key in a gangster's hand.

The skilled hands of the maid with clean, ironed sheets. Female students in love with a bachelor professor.

The municipal coffin with an old courtesan in it. The imagined rhythm of the footsteps of those who are not at the funeral but should, by a certain principle, bring at least a flower. She did so much for them.

Multiplication of needless things.

The uprooted stumps next tomuddy forklifts. Even pendulum amplitudesof the gilded wall clock...

Only through life, and even death, can we save ourselves from others. Every day I die within myself.

Dusting off a photograph of the deceased.

A chemical symbol on a peeled-off map of the Mendeleev's Periodic System.

My sister disappeared behind a row of figs. Lumps of words that would express my pain.

Climbing the wooden stairs with difficulty. That seems to be my destiny. Eyes tightly shut; I make an enemy of myself.

I'll start crying any minute now. Isn't it enough with these silly conversations already?

An unknown world of touching. Mother's lips pressed against the forehead of a child. She is waiting for it to fall asleep for someone is also waiting for her.

The ready and folded suitcase of the leaving and offended one.

Droplets of fat on the surface of a chilled soup.In a cup, a line from yesterday's tea that someone quickly gulped down.

Crucified iron Christ behind the locked gate of the cemetery. The closest tombstones - the last names of the most respected families. All the way in the corner, beneath the wall that divides the cemetery and the former furniture factory, in which everything was burnt to the ground, my mother's charred wooden mark. Only a few letters left of her. The former lady completely moved into me, though she knows it is tight here for both of us.

Ah.

9.

ONE MORNING J.M. had a hard time waking up. His nerves were baffled by the fact that his life was, practically, a thin thread, quite straight so as not to accidentally interfere with other threads, passed through endless streets and lives, complex sewage drains, and endless formulaic abstractions. All this is to be tightly braided into a thick flagellant's whip in his hands. He was about to wake up ... and already begin to calmly demolish the city.

It was a momentous decision at the instant he was not taking his eyes off of her while uttering too strong words for both of them. He offhandedly asked her to be polite so as not to make scenes in which he would recognize her neurotic behavior again.

A walk along the coast. One bed. Belgrade in the rain. Lilacs from the GospodarJevremova street. A few gloomy streets along the Danube Quay where his sadness takes a stroll. The fountainsin front of the Trade Union Hall under the November sky.

After all, the pitiless indifference erupting from him had led him into a state of superior self-awareness, which could not but additionally burden her.

What she wanted from him other than the fact that she had nothing to do with it and that she was not at all responsible for his so ruthless decision to leave her along with her daughter.

He is here far away from both his daughter and his wife and says nothing. The mister wears a ribbon over his left eye because he is doomed to become blind. His right eye is red as if he were using it just to cry. That skinny, dark face, worn-out rather than old. Speaks softly due to some heart disease.

I understand the reasons of your distress and your anger over the fact you've just found out – she spoke directly to his face – but your decision to leave us is tragically bold, defiant and emphatic, and you want to attach grandeur to everything, whereas it is infantile and comical, and eons away from being grand.

A naked little girl in front of the mirror. Clouds of bad music in the hotel lobby. Her half-naked body, skinny and weak, trembled beneath her skirt. I see nothing else but these eyes, these true eyes, these gorgeous eyes. Gentle murmur of blood in the beloved veins. A young woman witha mallow-colored face.

Surprisingly, he immediately agreed with her, but saying that he will always confirm his decision.

She stood before him strangely shaken and confused by his words, she was now careful not to look at him from the side, though she was tempted to do so. Until then she hadn't seen him like that, he had never stepped so outside himself. This was the reason she was so confused and terrified, standing now before an absolute stranger-beast, who, to say the least, was euphoric, tactless even towards himself and not just her. It made her so restless that she felt migraine blurring her vision.

This is pure masochism! This is pure madness! – she had nothing better to say.

With sadness treads the one who knows that life has deceived him. They tread side by side without turning their heads to each other. Opening his mouth like a pike. Under the purple lamp shade. Man strikes his balance where the tears, blood, flow of power, hair growth and the birth of laughter follow those same reliable laws at sea and the stars in the sky.

She shook her head left and right, I don't understand, I don't understand anything, had sin, carnality, lust, boredom, monotony been present in our marriage, I would have understood everything and not insisted on anything, it's over with Croatia, it's over with it, is that really what you wish? She fears that it is despair, that it is madness, that it is repressed self-pity and illusive solidarity with these unhappy people down there.

I will put my trust in God, in the country to which and the people to whom I go, and I will not regret if I make a mistake. You cannot understand this, and thank goodness for that. If I didn't leave, I would go insane here, since my place is no longer here. Life is one and short. You had your arguments for that, and I had mine.

Several trains, the speed of which undermines the landscape. Dying, lost in the pain of the clinic. The red loge of one theater. A narcissus meadow nearOpatija. A hand clutching a flower. The appeal of the minerals lined up in the museum showcase. Over the heavy and deep dark-green water, the intense color of which comes from the depths of the sea. Big waves of rough sea beat the sides of the boat.

Go where your stupid vanity takes you. Get out of my sight right away, because if you stay a moment longer, I could throw my arms around your neck and ask you to stay. If you cross the threshold, I don't want to either see you or hear from you, even if I were to croak because of such a cruel decision. It's only a reply to yours. Yours is cruel, mine is pathetic. The same goes for your daughters. Crossing the threshold of this flat, you close the door forever. "Put your trust in God, in the country to which and the people to whom you go?" Who do you think you are? Since when did you become God-fearing, a patriot and philanthropist?

I would have given my whole life if I had been able to put my hands on her temples and peel off her face like a mask. In front of me, in the little closet, I saw a pair of her old shoes with distorted heels. I would have squeezed with my arms and thighs that body loved more than God and more precious than my own life. I put her lifeless hands between my palms and tried to warm them, but they were frozen as if all the warmth of her body had gone into tears. Between two sobs, she confided in me that their baby had been alive but the doctors strangled it because it couldn't laugh. I saw bitterness in the corners of her lips as if she had constantly been swallowing misfortune. Her blue striped dress blinked as well as her colorless eyes as if someone had thrown dust in them. She looked at him persistently and maliciously.

I think you yourself know why I'm leaving;you're just pretending that it's not clear to you – he said. – This is not about quibbling, it's not the right word for the willingness to make the decision that preoccupies me all the more difficult for myself.

Brown horses, sorrel horses, horses somehow off-white, no hooves pounding, no neighing, no moans of death, in the absolute silence in which the cowboys were moving as they passed across the silent movie screen. She reminded him of a statue in the fountain. To her bent knees she lowers her open palms that still feel the weight of something lost. Her large ruffled black-and-white dress has the color of agitated sea waves. The heavy matter was falling from her hips to her feet and there, it was petrified in the form of a large stone wave, which matched and merged with the heaviness of the night. Her hands seemed to have come out from the dark sleeves, arrived from the unknown. They hovered in the air and as if they were there just to give a blessing.

He does not care whether she is a living woman or a statue. A single scar on the left descends to the corner of her serious lips, but this may be just a plain scratch he often saw on the bare scalps of porcelain dolls. She does not breathe, but her covered breasts and bare arms are immensely delicate and can belong only to a woman of flesh and blood.

At the same moment, he felt how everything was falling apartcompletely, everything that had been built between them for years, safe and reliable. Their paths were now diverging before their eyes and seeping somewhere into the porous soil.

The canal in which dead branches float. A basket full of snakes. A little window that is divided into four equal parts with cross-shaped bars. A nest of unprotected birds. A grave dug in the snow with candles burning out around it. His sex rests between the limbs with the purity of a sleeping child, his legs tightly clinging to one another look royal, like fallen pillars. Only one sandal tied to the foot, the toenails of which started to turn blue. The kitchen, a sink by the window, a table covered in oilcloth with black and white squares.

That same evening, with some luggage and a personal car, the manuscripts and books in cardboard boxes, he set off for Bosnia.

Apparently even by his own admission, he had for some time been following the dreadful path, which did not serve his self-possession and which he badly needed so that he would not, horrified, stare at the failure, against which he found salvation, and which moved him further upward but still did not go beyond his mental capacities. On such occasions, he found it a morbid pleasure to pursue conversations that he would lead with anyone about everyday or indifferent things. It was quite clear to him that these were attempts of escaping rather than the possibility of finding rest and recovery for himself.

For a long time, he sat reclined in a nonchalant and laid-back position on a wicker chair, his gaze becoming fixed so it seemed that he was lying in wait for something. His cheeks were flushed with an unpleasant blush thatoccurred as in a sudden sweep. The effect of his ultimate possibilities was limited, and for his understanding of such games it was, at the same time, terrifying as well. At the same time, he confronted a multitude of most different mood rhythms within himself which, as the time progressed, acquired distinctiveness and marvelous character, and thus he had to proceed with them from good-hearted amazement to utter acrimony, giving the whole conversation a rhythm of paradox, complacently indulging in the surf from the pious, serious and spiritual to mockery and hatred that were known to render threatening possibilities to the atmosphere, which is that things can very easily turn to a world of hell, a world of banality and commonplaces. His discourses mixed the analytical with the lyrical and had so much gentle energy and love, which he did not want to keep hidden within. It was this healthy speculation that guaranteed that he would eventually be dignified, because, in changing most various rhythms, he managed in some unusual way to maintain superior authority, while making those he talked to feel they understood him absolutely, and managed, in such a marvelous way, to keep in his mind the delusion that they, together with him, succeeded in changing most various rhythms in an unusual way and thus maintain superior authority over him.

A man and a woman walk slowly and talk in an undertone. They are her and him. They both look equally alive and equally dead. It is a rainy afternoon in which the pale glows of the day are reflected in the puddles. They interrupt their secretive subdued conversation. They are both dressed in dark-gray plain-cut clothes, slightly outmoded.

The whole horizon was reminiscent of the delicate, yet intense red wine tones.

He woke up from his dreamsullen, gloomy and depressed, but since he himself had forgotten the reasons for this miraculous condition, it often happened that he would suddenly emerge from some nightmare awakened by his own scream but without any memory of the danger that made him howl.

What dream will have a bad effect if dreamed over someone's beautiful shoulder, and then, it's sad to admit it: suffering and illness have altered his traits – he had no other solution but the odious and desperate one – to plunge into writing and to die a little just because he had no one to talk to about it...

10.

HOW DID FATHER disappear and when did his misfortune begin? How accustomed he was to the care and discomfort that he left us, though his status of a father had cost him a lot of effort, but also a lot of joy so that, at first, he handled it with ease and even more so, one might rightly say that he had enjoyed being able to perform all those nuisances with lightness and ease, day in day out. When he left – I found in one of his letters – that he had rid himself of the conflicts and passions that had mostly brought him uncertainty and worry. True, he still had a casual tendency to form some vague thought that would suddenly preoccupy him, but it apparently lasted very shortly for it did not worry him that much so as to make him pensive and upset. The abyss between him and others had almost disappeared, moreover, he had filled it every day, so he must have thought, and with good reason, that he had gotten over a few carved sculptures and made the whole thing short-lived and harmless, leaving them behind forever, by having hidden them behind the toilet bowl first, so that one fine day he would pick every single one up and throw them in the river. He had never felt relieved like that nor would he ever experience it again.

When he returned home from that tempest of feelings, and later relief, he was suddenly carried away by certain tenderness for mother, and then he was consumed with an absolute passion that made him – first – to get a pen and a piece of paper in the kitchen and write a poem as a paean to her body, and then go to the room where my mother and I slept and – lo and behold – he made that idiot Adri. He didn't even pay any attention to me, who climbed on his back and beat him with my little hands, thinking he was bashing or strangling mother, or what? And the two of them just cracked up at me, my tears and my fear that dad would kill mom. "You see, luv, that mom is not angry, she's laughing" - those two animals assured me.

In one of the letters was the manuscript of that poem.

Her eyes are two volcanic craters,
Smoke is steaming out of her nostrils,
Her mouth are two reefs of the coral,
Her hair sweeps the road she walks.

Her breasts are the two white oriels,
Her gaze is by the Sun conducted,
For her hips the pathway is tight,
As on pillars she holds her edifice.

She's a natural treasure of the planet,
Which fetes before my very eyes,
Ain't she stunning, Goddamn her,
Quake itself wouldn't plow through her.

In dad's letters from those years, which were not many anyway or a number of them got lost, an irrepressible urge to explore could be seen, at the basis of which lay some of his former doubts about his roots. In the more sublime sense of the word, his understanding of the scheme of these roots was precisely defined there, on which, indeed, a keen eye could read all sorts of things between the lines and pretty easily reach a conclusion on certain matters. Probably, and not without admiration, in his behavior he endeavored to overcome the constant feeling of alienation, anxiety and escalating excitement, whether he was thinking of former Bosnian heretics, or learning about his relationship with Aman Fanny, and he was no less attracted to his boxes with manuscripts which, he was sure already then, would never see the light of day, but not because of someone's sloppiness, neglect and disregard, but because they did not deserve it at all. He was pleased with a feeling that he knew what beauty was, although he had not been able to put it on paper the way he understood it. For this, he quickly made connections with people who could be of use to him, but he grew cold towards these individuals even quicker, as too soon they would start to bore him, making his good-natured patience more and more out of breath, and–it seems, their own too – to help him in such his disorientation.

Moreover, his distrust of others spread to his own self-esteem over time. The occasions were such that he left more and more time to talk to himself and to try to remove the threatening part of the unknown from his face, which appeared in the mirror. He already had a bit of premonition of this ominous game in his youth, sensing that it might hit him later in life. One uncorroborated story, yet convincing enough to be easily believed, dated back to that time. Namely, in front of the mirror in the school restroom, one of his students, prone to buffoonery, mimicked before the adolescents how Professor Melez was absolutely always aware of all his moves, whether viewed from profile or en face, which, of course, given the nature of the work, can be taken as a standard of professional taste, but also as a considerable touch of affectation. Rumor had it that Professor J.M. practiced for each class in front of the mirror, which he put in different positions so that he could see himself from every possible angle in the classroom. He equally regarded both, the most hidden gaze of that most negligent student and the one from the most orthodox nerd, sitting in the first row of the middle line, next to the very teacher's desk. Except for a certain lack of the sense of humor in this adolescent buffoonery, it must be noted by that, after all, there was a flicker of admiration and gratitude in the air for his alleged propensity. Again, it is about the alleged propensity, which holds that the Professor's passion to be liked by everyone was an end in itself.By the way, it should be pointed out that he built his authority and power in spite of his benevolent and conciliatory nature, and because of this he had a few supporters who practically adored him, but goodness knows, on the other hand, malicious tongues spoke of all sorts of stuff and added some more. It is a true luck that dad had never been used or tormented by curiosity, so all of that gibberish failed to reach his ears. This did not prevent the former from admiring him even more and adding a plus and this virtue of his on his account just as it did not stop the latter to speak even more ill of him, not seeing that they were lost in the fruitless condemnation of a man who neither bothered nor wanted to bother anyone, perhaps only excluding himself from that combination.

When Professor J.M. was finally warned of becoming the object of mockery for his *hamming in the classroom*, and finally became aware that this remark was not that morning's news but had to have been rolling and blowing up for quite some time with the bitterness and unhealthy scorn on the lips and in the hearts of these immature spirits, he carefully and soberly examined his position and his ability to change it. Even then, he had to admit to himself that doing such a job had already tired him out, and even exhausted him, so that he reached the point when he could not go any further, or do anything more, but could only slide on, which he would not, under any circumstances, agree to or accept such compromise. In fact, that compromise would be equal to his defeat, which, after all, his pride and dignity could never agree on.

Over time, this service became more and more of a burden and less of a joy, especially now that he had lived to hear even a remark to his latest gag by which he tried to cast some other color and illumination on the issues. Per his wishes at the time, it would have been better had he remained unnoticed than to have suddenly found himself in the limelight. Instead of intensifying his pursuit of finding new joys in the classroom, he was now forced to defend himself and to justify himself for what he himself otherwise thought little of, except the fact that he thus eliminated boredom that had started bothering him the most in this line of work. He just could not understand why there was so much hatred and aversion to him; he allegedly undermined authority of all other professors to have his own rise to divine heights. Indeed, he himself had to respond to such nonsense with a tortured smile.

What an astuteness! Ah, what an astuteness!

Finding in this rudeness a *live true life*, he thought with great resignation that he began to understand that this *live true life*was not for him, and that he was not capable of fighting the magnetic forces of such*live true life*, and he had to find other means that would, like a shell, protect him against external inconveniences. True, he admitted, it would be a cowardly and under-the-lee vegetation, and without many heavy duties with day-to-day, tedious and boring orientations.

Pulling out one letter at random from a pile, I noticed a piece of paper written-on in purple ink and unknown handwriting. It most surprised me since I knew that my father had no friends, at least not so intimate that he might have corresponded with them. I was unable to contain my excitement; the lines almost began to mix before my eyes. Like a flash of lightning, a hunch shot through me. In order to prepare myself and be a match for what my tormented soul expected, I closed my eyes over the spread paper, and instead of breathing in as much air as I would need to come back to my senses at least a bit, I actually completely abandoned myself to dejection, seeking peace in such kind of balance.

Is there a better way to start again with the new cycle of grief and melancholy? I opened the door to my spirit and let the icy atmosphere of loneliness settle in it.

The very beginning of this letter unsettled and moved me.

My beloved friend!

Threat, imploration, promise, humility, or what?

I sat and listened. I was trying to absorb these secrets by opening up all the pores of my skin. It was almost unnecessary to prove that to this day I remained clueless about the missing link, which further reinforces my doubts, or even then I started leaning towards the thought that life is a great and never-resolvable mystery in which we put away our undefined fears for safekeeping.

During our last encounter, I had a lot to tell you, but at one point I realized that words are not as sensitive as our innermost feelings. Expressed in mathematical terminology: words do not complement human nature and the instincts, which the enlightened spirits are ashamed of as something that is inherent to animals. What if, despite the civilizational desire to differentiate ourselves from them by using shame as punishment, seeking for the meaning, having a sense of beauty, we are still what we have always been, except that we have used words to lie and hide ourselves. We have become estranged from each other lately, which troubles me even more through the fact that I am preventing myself from truly understanding you. I'm afraid the reason is that some of your thoughts have been too liberal and abstract that I did not measure up to them. True, I must admit, they were within my reach, but the path I took did not lead me to the point of being pleased with how I solved their enigma. The few variants that presented themselves, eventually, led me to a dead end.

For the fear of doing wrong, I have not gladly yielded to seduction. Paying closer attention, I tried not to inconvenience father in relation to what I felt for him. I sensed the plants, animals, and earth trembling with me, the pink light lingering in the sky to keep on illuminating the space around me. Through a fraction of the window pane, with somerestlessness, I was watching that transfigured and cursed sky, which was now grinning at me and leaving its light to bare me as much as possible if by any chance I became aware of the horror and if before that the earth had not swallowed me.

A melancholic mood caused by home loneliness and peace led me to the crazy idea of getting into writing again. And then, as I found myself in complete scarcity and shortage as far as any matter was concerned, I offered myself as content and subject. Hence this story has a strange and awkward plan, and there is nothing worth noticing in it except the perverse. A woman loves herself most when she is the least right. I know I'm not the former, and that I'm probably the latter.

I wandered, losing my mind from the beauty and sadness of the scene, from the trees leaning over the water, from the broken images in the water, from the beggars on the moldy church porches, from the scent of strawberries and blackberries in the market. The sky the color of the rose, from which the ruffled clouds had cleared, the spooky trees endlessly stretched. Magnificent silence, closed eyelids, bolted shops.

It became clear to me that everything had spread – toresist such fate would be the same as stopping the wind with your hands. The body understood this eons ago, but my spirit did not want nor was able to comprehend it. For days I was in a kind of subdued madness from despair. I tried not to preempt anything in advance, but in vain, the only thing to do is to put my finger across my lips once more and to remain silent. I no longer had the strength, not even for a mocking smile.

There, merciful God, what a spectacle you created for your own fun!

I sighed once more with a heavy heart, and with my best effort I got on the floor and surrendered to the solitary exercises of humiliation and penance, which I will not give up until I feel in that same heart the cold and ruthlessness when, perhaps, peace in my tormented soul will again be established. One needs to believe, God, because you are absolutely good, even though you are absolutely perfect and absolutely glorious in yourself, you created the world from nothing so that other perfections too, glorifying You, may participate in Your goodness. You created everything for Your sake, and for Your sake everything exists.

11.

THE NEWS OF Aman Fanny's death was learned only in the morning. The TV-payment collector stood at the front door for a while, he called her twice, then looked at his watch, not believing she could have gone to the store so early. He was just about to leave when a cast-off female slipper caught his attention. Just then, he heard the hissing of the television that had no program on except for the snow on the screen. This seemed significant to him. He stood on the spot for an instant or two, and then called Aman Fanny for the third time.

No one answered him this time either. How could a spirit like his not encompass this thing as well? In his excitement he was already more than just curious, therefore he must have taken a step at the moment when he had already made up his mind, so that he would not be overly surprised.

His hand clutched at the handle, and opening the door ever so slightly was enough for him to instantly see Aman Fanny, crumpled on the floor.

The television screen was hissing in vain.

It would be irrelevant to say anything about surprise on his part, but what he had suspected with some sort of fear before himself sobered him up pretty quickly. Now he had to bend down to see if her tongue was really slit. It could be seen on his face that it was not easy for him, he was seized by horrible disgust, and his watery blue eyes widened even more, so he ran outside, tense-faced, to look for someone in the neighborhood.

It is simply impossible to describe the degree of delight that stood out of the seriousness with which the next-door neighbor of the deceased had done the most urgent things before the doctor arrived with the team. Everything was mixed here: from compassion, discretion, awe, all the way to petty-bourgeois timidity and pathos in the face of death. Obviously, she was imbued by the thought of belonging to a world of knowledge and suffering.

After all, while she was doing this, the strangely distressing details of conversations with late Aman Fanny kept popping up before her, in which conversations she for the first time revealed her feelings, except that this time they were melting away in an almost malicious pleasure that had to be somehow subdued and concealed. She could remember the myriad of these details that, to her, in her somewhat detached consciousness seemed mixed up and abstract, and, besides taming her momentary affection for the deceased, something instinctively swelled in her, say, something like the fear that this hateful and disgusting woman might suddenly wake up and see her above herself. It was not her ordinary affectation or the flirtation of the living over the dead, but the most serious craze that she herself would occasionally brood about. It can be seen in the deepening of her wrinkles between her eyebrows, and the expression of confused guesswork that is passing over her face.

Once again, she wanted to make sure that Aman Fanny had indeed died, so she surreptitiously turned her head a bit, and thanked dear God most kindly and humbly, now quite exhausted, half-distressed, half self-pityingly shaken.

A few days later, in the middle of the night, the sirocco started blowing and slammed the wooden shutters against the wall. The woman was startled awake from her first sleep and saw it as a bad omen.

Something was rattling nearby.

She had to muster up all the courage to overcome the fear she felt splashing her like waves and leaving in her an impression of the bottomless pit in which she would soon sink without hope.

That damn mug of hers is banging, she thought. They forgot to take it off the tap.

In her mind, the memory of Aman Fanny, with whom she had been in constant squabbles for seven years, came to life. She constantly feared that her neighbor would outlive her, and that she would leave this world she had blessed every day and would have blessed it even more had Aman Fanny not completely made her life miserable with the daily threats, from burning her house along with her at night to the point that she would somehow enter her house to kill her in her sleep.

The reason was quite mundane: a patch of garden to which Aman Fanny claimed entitlement, because she had somehow managed with bribe to have it registered in the local cadaster in her own name, while the neighbor considered it her ancestral propertysince time immemorial. To make the issue more complicated, both women were distant cousins through their fathers.

Basically, the truth was that Aman Fanny's neighbor became a bundle of nerves. Aman Fanny kept talking to the chickens by the fence, telling them that they could be happy because they were chickens since people were heavy thieves, liars and bastards.

Hidden in a summer kitchen, her neighbor remained silent and listened to the cackling of chickens that meant they agreed with Aman Fanny's conclusion.

- It's clear both to you and to the One up there whose garden this is – she heard what Aman Fanny was saying to the chickens.

Evenings were even more painful. Aman Fanny used to climb to the terrace, turn the tap on the fountain that would shake because of the vacuum in the water pipes, and pour it into a porcelain mug. She would then collect saliva in her mouth and spew briefly towards her neighbor's house.

It's understandable that these moments were etched in the mind of the frightened woman, and she, now, sought to remove them from her memories. She had already shown a strong inclination to give it all up, to withdraw from the world of people, and thus stopped receiving any guests, fearing that Aman Fanny would use them to sneak into her flat and play a dirty trick on her. She completely limited her widow's life to the kitchen and the room above it.

Besides all that, she was still peevish and rueful. She acted with extreme caution, which made her life even more anxiety-ridden, along with the fact that she had completely left all social circles in which she had been active and had received some important acknowledgments from them until then.

She became listless and curt, constantly grumbling and complaining about her fate, but she dared not confide in anyone so that it would not reach Aman Franny's ears, for that witch would surely have puffed up for having been able to scare her with the threats.

She expressed her averseness to such a life even towards her pet parrot, to which one day she thoughtlessly opened the cage door and simply let it fly away. She didn't even allow herself to shudder when the bird flitted away.

She had had enough of everything.

And later came *that* as well. She was only afraid that she would scream with joy in front of those present, and later in front of the doctor, and embrace them all. She was even afraid that this scream might wake the witch from her sleep, so she decided to restrain and conceal herself, and to calm down.

The mug still rattled, hitched to the tap handle.

They forgot to take it off the tap.

The rattling from the terrace continued. What she couldn't let go of and yet in a sense had reconciled herself to, and what, shaking her head constantly, she was also amazed at, was certain flaunting audacity of that mug, which with her rattle mimicked Aman Fanny's voice: "Sooner or later, I'm gonna get you!"

-Am I imagining this? – into the darkness, her face pressed against the glass.

The rattle was still coming from there.

- Is her soul hiding in that mug? Maybe her apparition will come out of the mug any minute? If I continue to look in that direction, it will really happen in the end.

Instead of looking away from the window, she reached out for the door handle to open it and to better see that mug, so as to convince herself that it was really that ordinary porcelain mug with two painted puppies opposite each other and with a chipped circle under the ear of one of them.

That same instant, the wind slammed the frames so powerfully that the glass broke. The cup appeared before her eyes, but this time huge as a barrel, and those two dogs barked at each other: "You thought?"

- You're dead! – yelled the woman, pushing her body forward through the broken window.

She felt the force of the wind on her glowing cheeks. Tears were welling up in her eyes while her body was shaking with unbridled laughter.

The next day they found her on the ground. No one was able to say why the unhappy woman had her teeth clenched.

12.

I TRY TO be indifferent so as to silence my own doubts, which – again –seem to bear something forbidden and ugly within. Besides, it was necessary to devote myself to the inconvenience of digging into other people's lives, which, admittedly, was below my dignity, but some devil was making me do that, and I was somewhat ashamed, indeed, feeling some discomfort. We are used to women blushing as soon as something is mentioned, which they are happy to do. I scratched my head with one finger like a man who thereby unconsciously reveals that he has just been discovered. The terrible fear of defeat made me more upset than the defeat itself.

Although, before the walk, father had listened carefully and quite gladly to my words, on other occasions, again, he used to exhibit aversion and spite. In that, I sensed some of his power, not only towards me but also towards everyone around him, which in our further relationship could be dangerous so I could soon show him the worse side of my character.

I was once telling him how at a summer resort a few months earlier I had experienced an inconvenience by playing, like most kids did, *dad and mom* with one little boy in the bush, when suddenly another boy approached and shouted at us:"Yuck!"

Father was quiet, still sitting in the statue position, radiating with serenity and silence, so for that reason only I wished to keep telling him for a while about what happened to me afterwards. I could never have guessed that my mother and father would so easily pass over this confidential divulgence of mine. By the way, they even tried to teach me that there was no harm in that. Still, I was ashamed and instead masturbated before bedtime.

One night, in the late summer, I was returning home from a local work action where about twenty pioneers participated. Along the way we sang a multitude of songs about Tito. And then I met the gaze of an old woman who was just passing by, and I instantly shivered because of her eyes, which in and of themselves were not beautiful at all like those of noble people, and they also indicated that they neither knew nor acknowledged the sins of youth. A moment later, a rather ironic thought flashed across my mind that this old woman might be the witch from the fairy tale of Hansel and Gretel.

Be that as it may, that crow's gaze of hers almost completely brought me back from certain sweet intoxication of that primitive world within me, especially as I struggled, by the way, to maintain the balance since we drank some beer, when I heard her hysterically shouting at us: "Godless gang, may the devil take you all to hell!"

My first sense of doubt and desire to see myself in a light that would probably not bring me good mood, I expressed that same night when, alone in bed, I wanted to masturbate again, and that's when, for the first time, I felt that there must be someone above us, who watches over us, seduces us, destroys us and opens for us the paths of hope again.

God. He sees and punishes. Couldn't he have hidden himself in the figure of that old woman by sending his spirit into hers, and then, by the same token, I remembered my experience with that boy in the bush. I stopped rubbing my clitoris between my fingers, imagining myself under him. Such behavior probably had its reasons. I sensed that something important and something serious was about to happen, perhaps not as beautiful, some widening or narrowing of my horizon, which, of course, led me into even more confusing dilemma, temptation and danger. I was afraid that I would not be able to understand these contradictions, and I feared that I would be too weak and too inexperienced for something like that.

The dream came as a salvation, but the awakening was the one that brought me true salvation and excitement due to the nightmare, which suddenly and strangely shook me so much so that, awaken, I was in tears for a long time. I thought: so, I really died in this dream, and now, behold, I am alive again. We couldn't really govern this, now, could we?

I had to remember what excited me so much. And I remember the great light and God opening the heavens and inviting me to come up to Him...

If I were to write anything else, I would have to make it up, so I will stay only with the image mentioned. I read somewhere that summer dreams are true.

I think one should pay attention to how one lives one's life. If reincarnation happens, one will be what one he had deserved to be. I think in my future life I will be a fly and live very briefly.

I am contemplating the way of dying. My decision is that it be something fast, say, jump off an airplane without a parachute.

CHAPTER THREE

P. S.

Love

NO ONE EXPECTED such a thing, nor could have imagined that this elderly man would be able to do such a thing.

God forbid!

Could it really have been him, or was it someone else banging the church bell with a hammer at night; someone younger, so one would somehow even understand such after-midnight wantonness. The foolishness of youth, so what can you do? We used to be like that too; some more, some less.

Hence no one could think of, or hold for truth, what in fact he himself saw with his own eyes and heard with his own ears: an old man on the church tower frantically thrashing the bell.

It goes without saying that the police immediately took the matter into their own hands. The moment when the bell first sounded could not be determined with certainty. It could be said, therefore, that a few accidental eyewitnesses had completely disagreed in what they had sworn to the investigator, which, of course, completely changed the meaning of their testimony, notwithstanding their cynical remarks, which sought to persuade him that their story was not a figment of imagination but a hundred-percent truth.

I'd have to be completely crazy to fall for something like this, thought the young investigator. So, I can't even think to blindly trust their words.

He rightly suspected that none of them had managed to conceal from him certain jealousy over the old man's affair with an unknown woman; he would, therefore, let them know that their jealousy was something common and conspiratorial that linked them in their testimony against this man, allegedly for the disruption of public order and peace of citizens.

XY had led a practically withdrawn life by then. It wasn't like that: a mere hearsay. Such belief had originated even earlier, if only conditionally and as a realistic possibility.

The investigator was most amazed and perplexed that he refused, with such smooth persistence, to say who the female he had been with that night was. To pay a fine or to spend a few days in jail, he had completely reconciled to it, accepting it from the first moment as a normal consequence of what he had done. Of course, he expected that by then his regular, or rather, nonexistent sex life would bring him at least a pitying smile, or even be a mitigating circumstance. He maintained that he would not tell on the female.

Every female was under suspicion. Most of them, raising a hue and cry against the old man, insisted that he deserved to have that thing cut off. Some remained silent and frowned, hoping that they would look less suspicious to their husbands and other people.

J.M. himself did not worry much about it, not even when his own ears heard that he, the poor wretch, had made it all up, or, even worse, that he had imagined such thing really happening to him.

- Maybe, J.M., you dreamt about it?

- Maybe?

He continued, without beating around the bush, with lustfulness, to talk about all the details of how he had gone to bed early that night, as usual somewhere after the TV News, how he'd just gotten in bed, opened the book, *A Time of Death*novel by DobricaĆosić, been on page 154, and then suddenly there was a knock on the door. He was surprised that someone was knocking on his door at that hour, so he stood still on the spot and began listening for who could that be in the dead of the night. He wanted to ask the one outside the door who he was and what he wanted, but held himself back and decided to wait a bit longer for the knocking to be repeated.

The knocking happened once more, his heart was pounding, he just had to reach out and turn the key in the lock, twice to the left.

His astonishment when he really did that and opened the door. Standing on the threshold was – she!

- May I come in? – she asked him.

I don't know how I permitted her in: I either nodded or moved aside or told her something, the devil only knows, basically, she passed by me and I just remembered to look quickly down the hall to see if someone else was with her.

I chewed overher unusual manner of entering the flat. I had to deal with the feeling that this did not impress me in the slightest, though I was already going over things with extreme caution, linking them to her possible intentions.

In rapture and doubt, my heart was pounding frantically. I couldn't allow my feelings to betray me due to her sudden visit, thus I was so confused that, fool, I even forgot the simplest house rule of offering her a chair. Willfully quietly and seemingly uninterestedly, Iasked the first thing that came to my mind. She was smiling at me; she had to see that her arrival made a huge impression on me.

The woman was quite familiar. My soul was stirred with excited expectation, curiosity, exaltation and anxiety, casting me into deep rapture and trance.

He made no secret that, once having given herself to him, she would live in peace only for a moment, only for now, until she had redeemed herself sufficiently before her husband, he would ask her again and again whenever he would want her to show her gratitude for his silence, which he would break if she denied him, just like she would deny that gratitude if he were to break his silence. From now on, the two of them would have to live in adultery.

If her waywardness would become known, she will still have had a mockery of her morals, and now, along with adultery, it seemed to be an integral part of the decoration of her life.

Although he felt more confused than uncomfortable, he knew, and knew all too well, that he had to immediately engage in the joyful cognition of what there was, which then automatically meant consent without any hesitation. It even occurred to him to suggest: if we would be serious for a moment, but he instantly admitted to himself that something like that would be absolutely stupid.

It happened then that for a moment he was headed to experience a humongous shame, so he alone didn't know what to think about himself. Contrary to all expectations, he did not act properly, and by no means was he able to properly do his job upon such a sudden and unexpected offer, which made him rage furiously, and he was even afraid that she would laugh in his face and leave, though she kept whispering to him, why are you upset, calm down, everything will be fine, you'll see. Don't tell me you haven't shagged anyone so far?

And then the church bell was heard from afar, his self-confidence returned immediately. She first caressed his hand, then put it next to his, keeping them side by side, and then her hand slid towards his tool, rubbed it several times, it instantly started to grow, he felt the impending passion and bulging strength, indeed still gentle and timid, but already such that he turned her away from him, then laid her face-down, and clasped his hands around her waist, kneading her huge jugs, which were swinging like the Sunday bells of Notre-Dame, he flung her to the ottoman, she seemingly tried to calm him down, but he lifted her dress spraying spermlike from a fire hose all over herbefore slamming his heavy howitzer in-between her legs all the way to her larynx, and when she compared him to a horse, he started crying out of happiness, like a baby.

After that he thought: until this very moment, he had not touched any woman, now a woman touched him.

Maks took his paws off her, removed that tool of his that looked like the end of a wet rope, and put it back in its lair. Then he ran out of the flat, grabbing a hammer from the drawer on the way.

The haughtiness of the spirit, hot blood, curiosity, vanity and desire made him run like crazy. That feeling still had a hold on him when he climbed up the steel rope to the church bell, and even when he swung his hammer at it. First, one powerful blow, then fifty-three stronger and weaker blows by turns. In the end, Maks screamed like an Indian and raised the hammer as if it were a tomahawk.

Sarajevo, 23 January 2017

Lightning Source UK Ltd.
Milton Keynes UK
UKHW010706240520
363742UK00004B/117/J

9 781984 594884